A FOREWORD

IT HAS BEEN MANY YEARS SINCE VOLUME ONE WAS RELEASED AND AS A RESULT, MANY ARTISTIC STYLES HAVE CHANGED AND GROWN. IT HAS BEEN A FUN JOURNEY, BUT STILL ALWAYS CHANGING AND WILL BE EXCITING TO SEE HOW MY WORK DEVELOPS MORE IN THE FUTURE!

THIS BOOK CONTAINS ART BETWEEN 2018-2020, FROM PERSONAL PIECES, COMMISSIONS, AND BOTH A LONG FORM AND A FEW ONE PAGE COMICS.

I HOPE YOU ENJOY AND IF YOU'RE CURIOUS FOR MORE, CHECK OUT OTHER BOOKS FURPLANET PRINTS OR EVEN SCAN THE QR CODE FOR MY GALLERIES AND SOCIALS.

SINCERELY,
KAYLII

LINKTR.EE/KAYLIIMAE

PUBLISHED BY FURPLANET

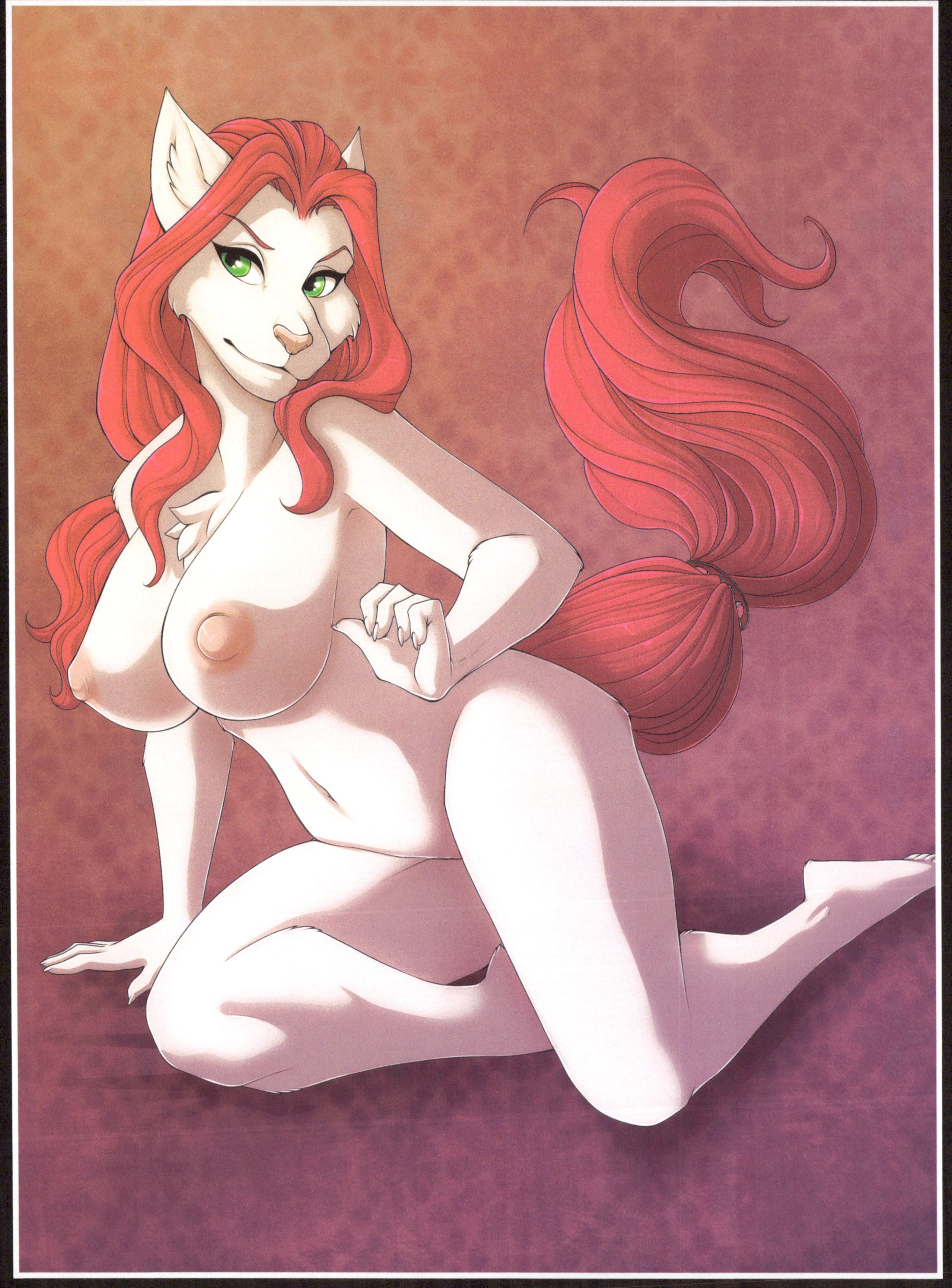

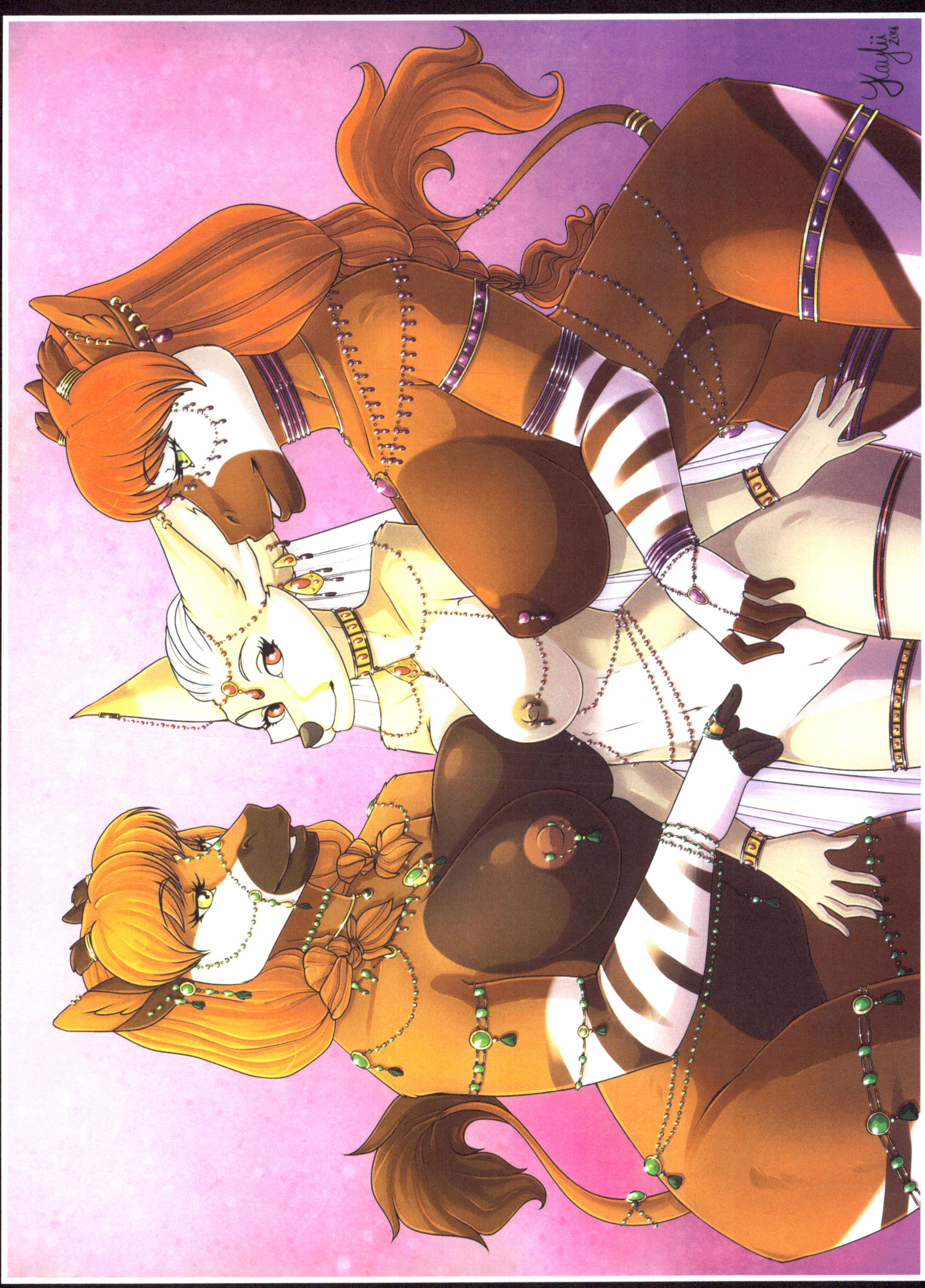

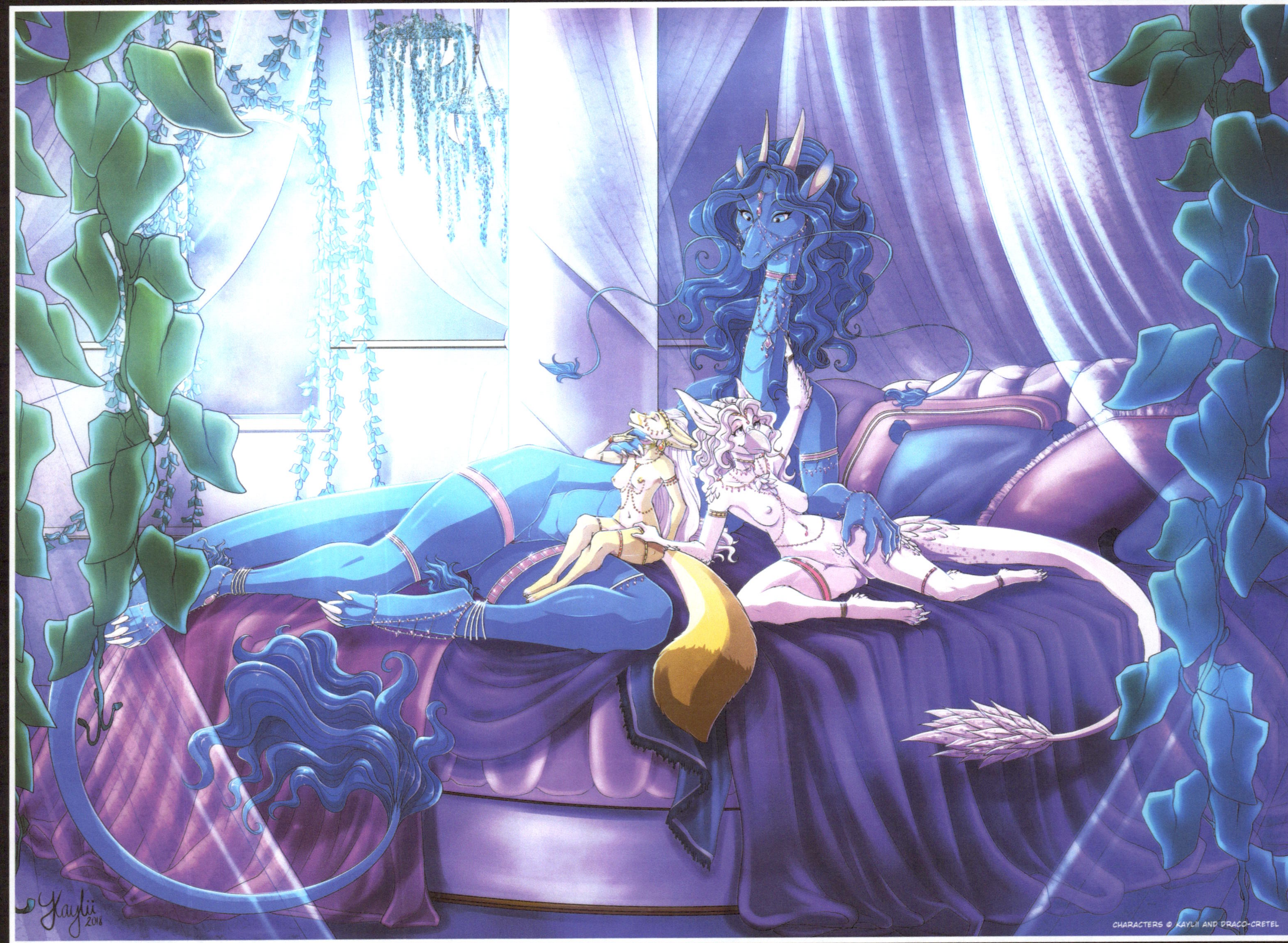
CHARACTERS © KAYLII AND DRACO-CRETEL
Kayliï 2018

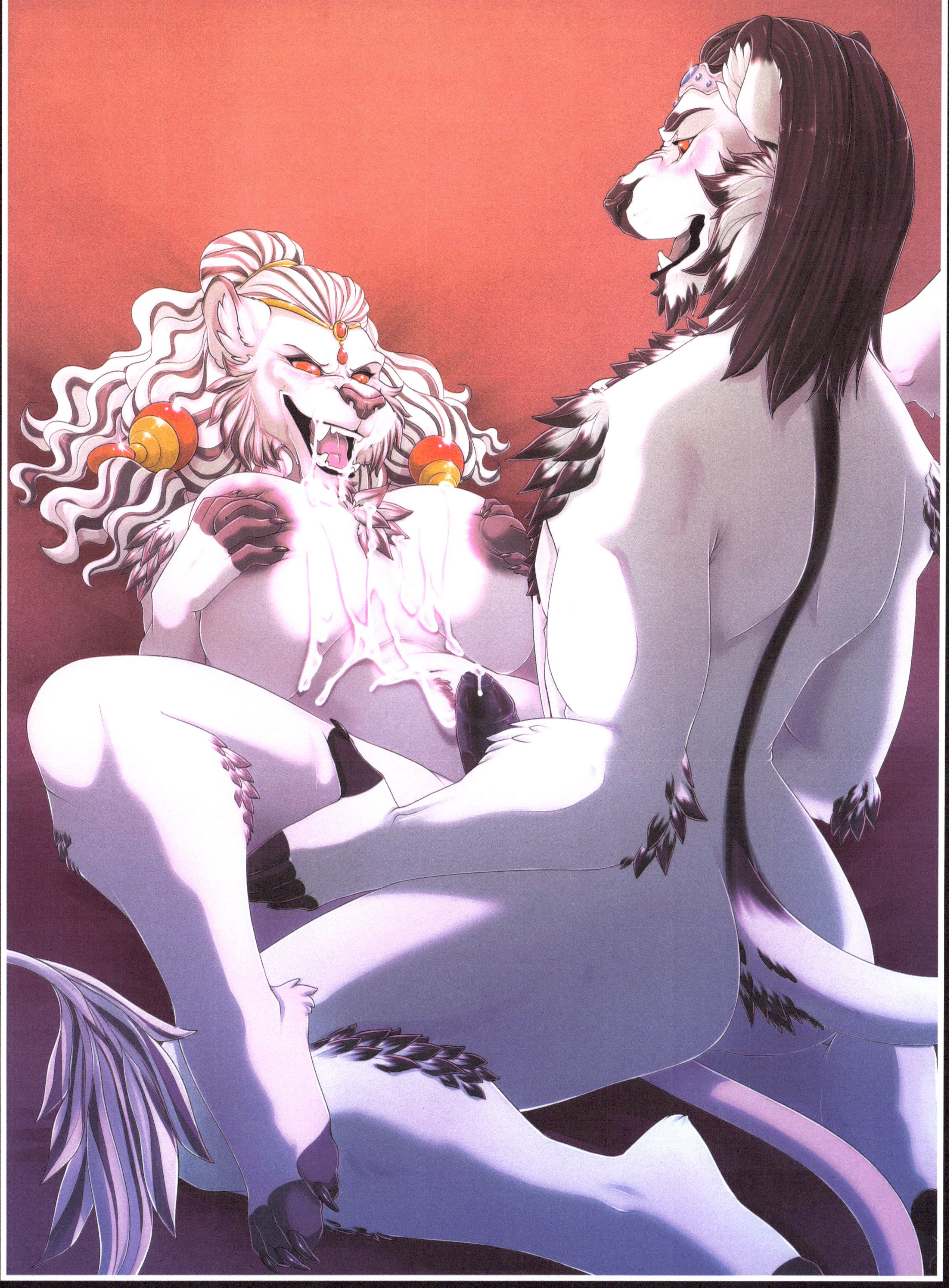

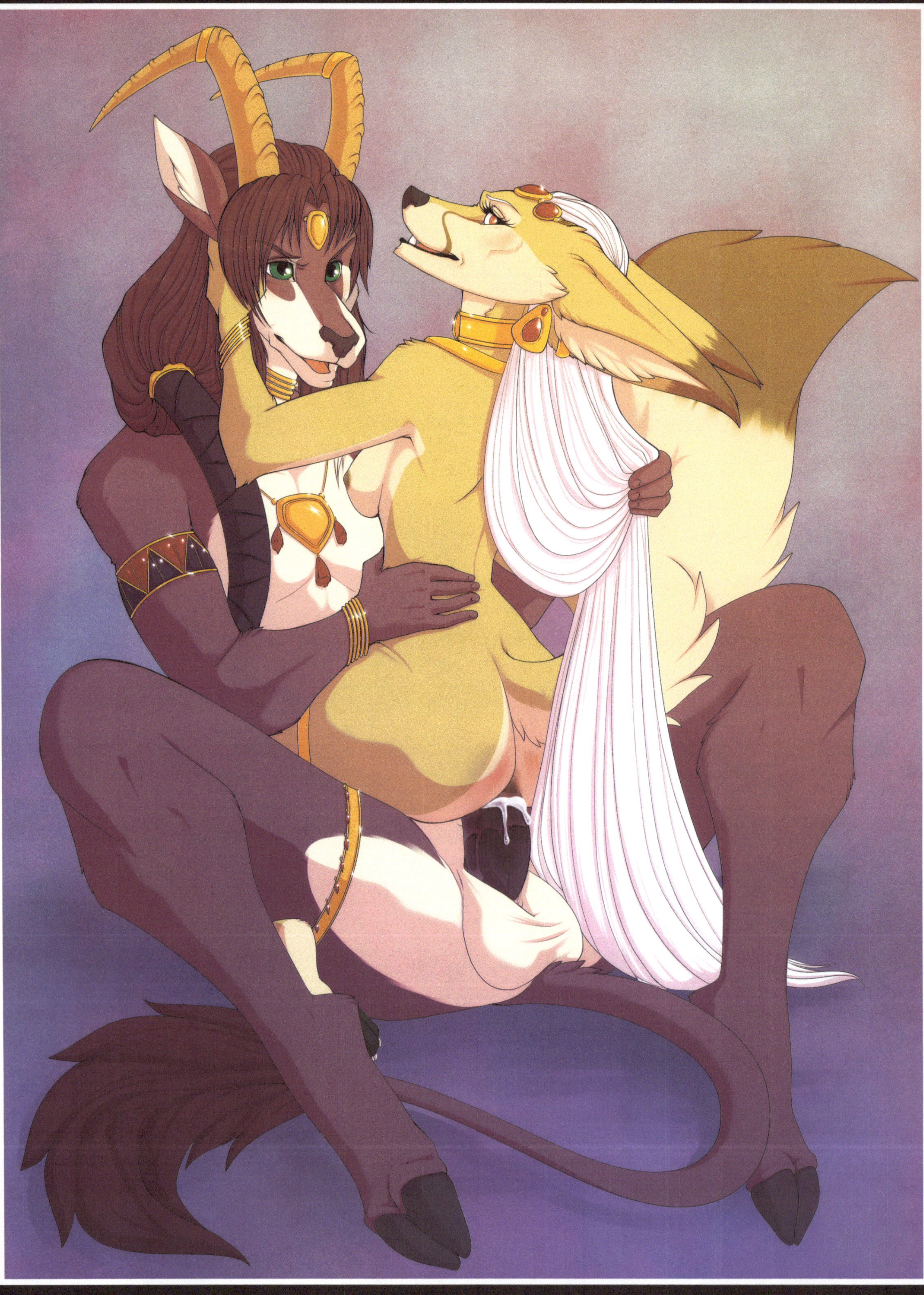

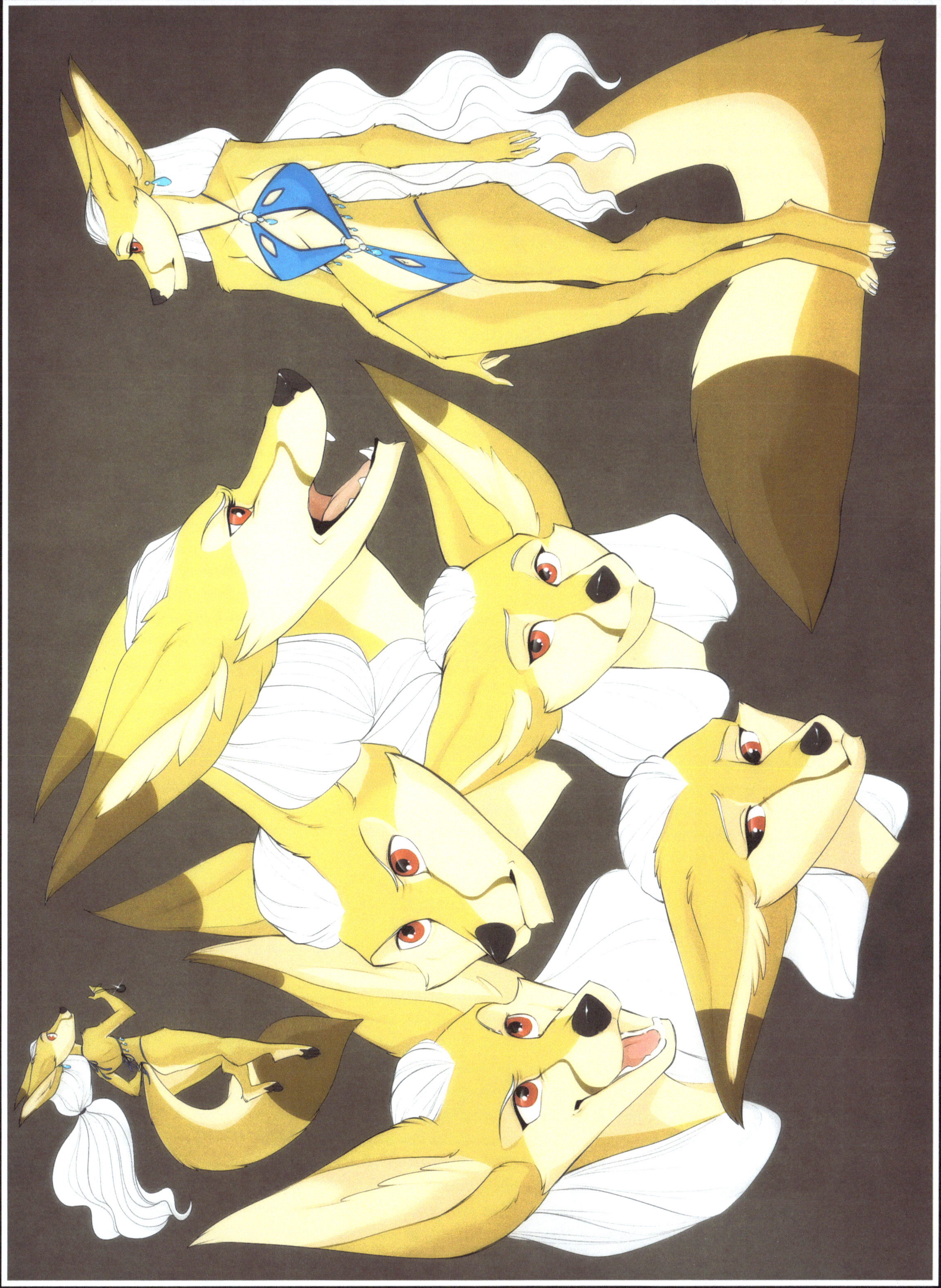

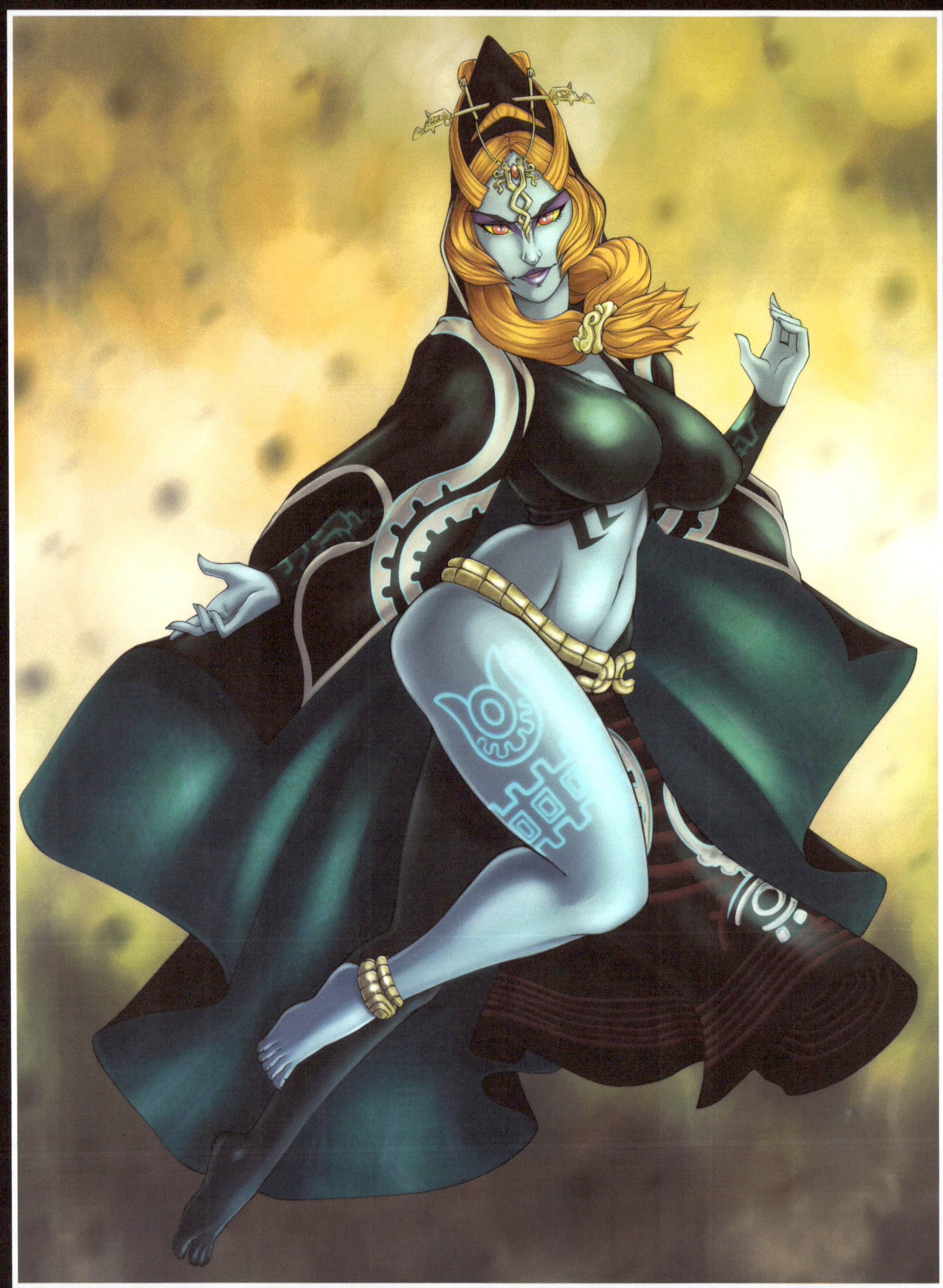

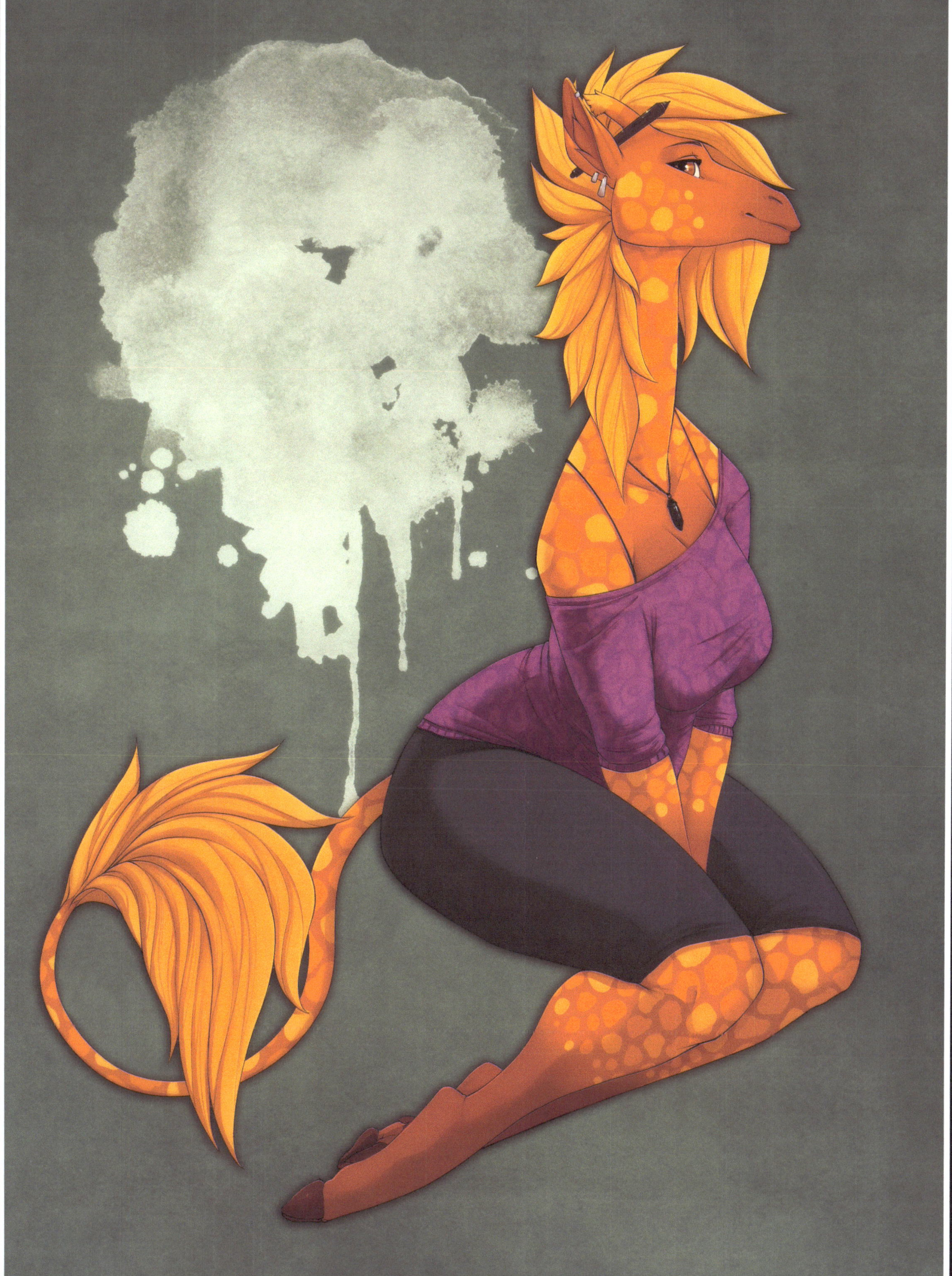

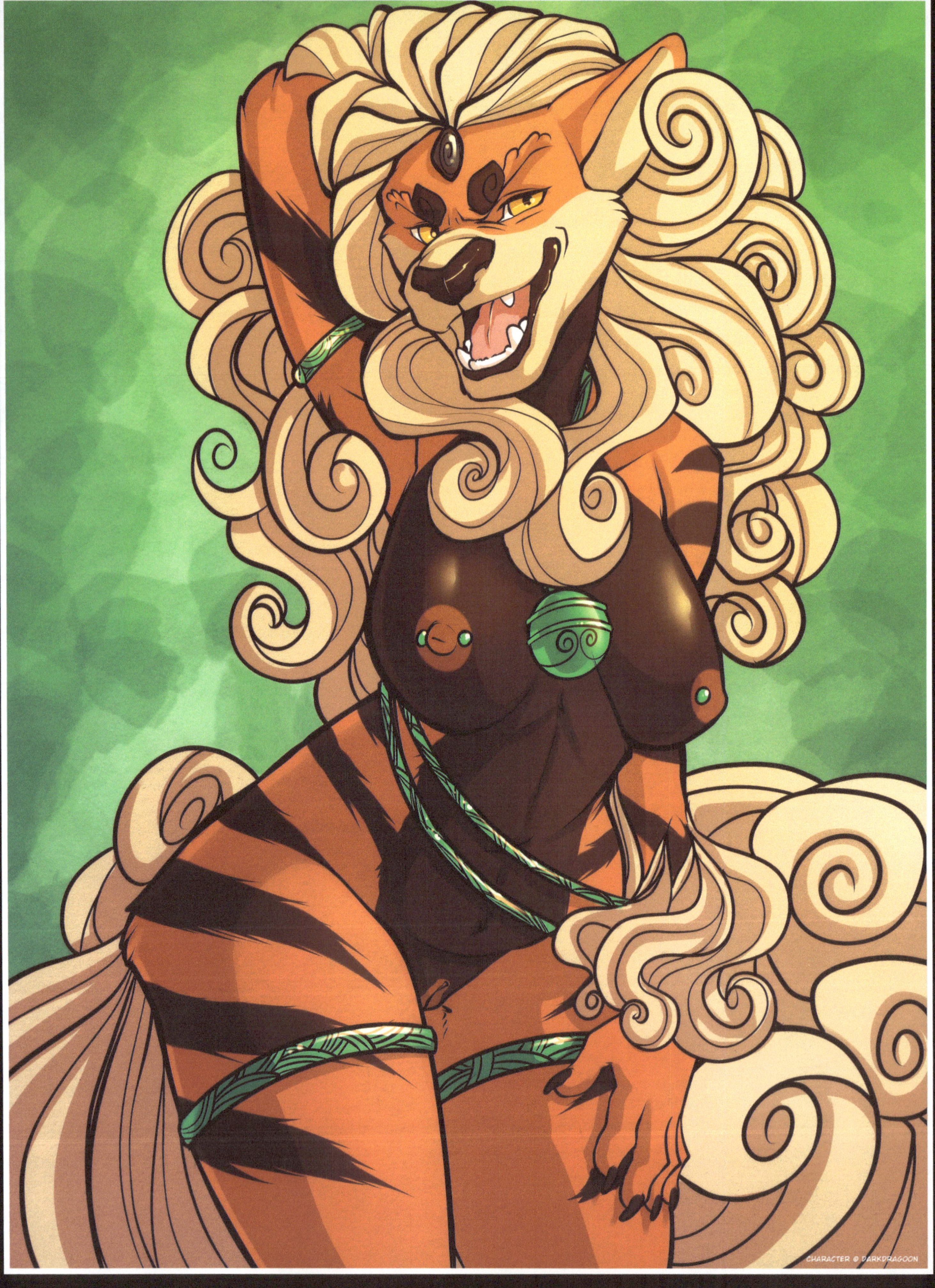
CHARACTER © DARKDRAGOON

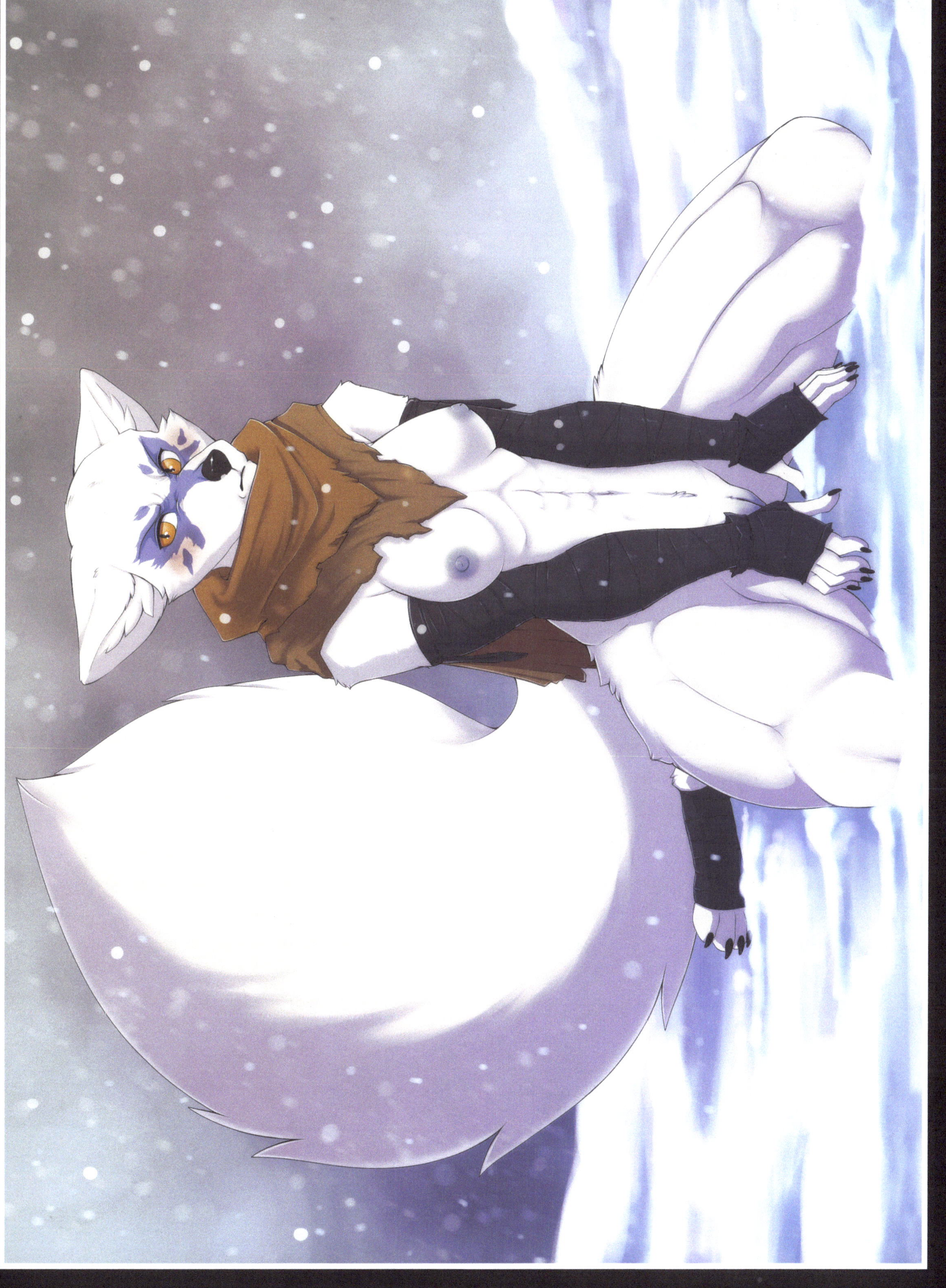

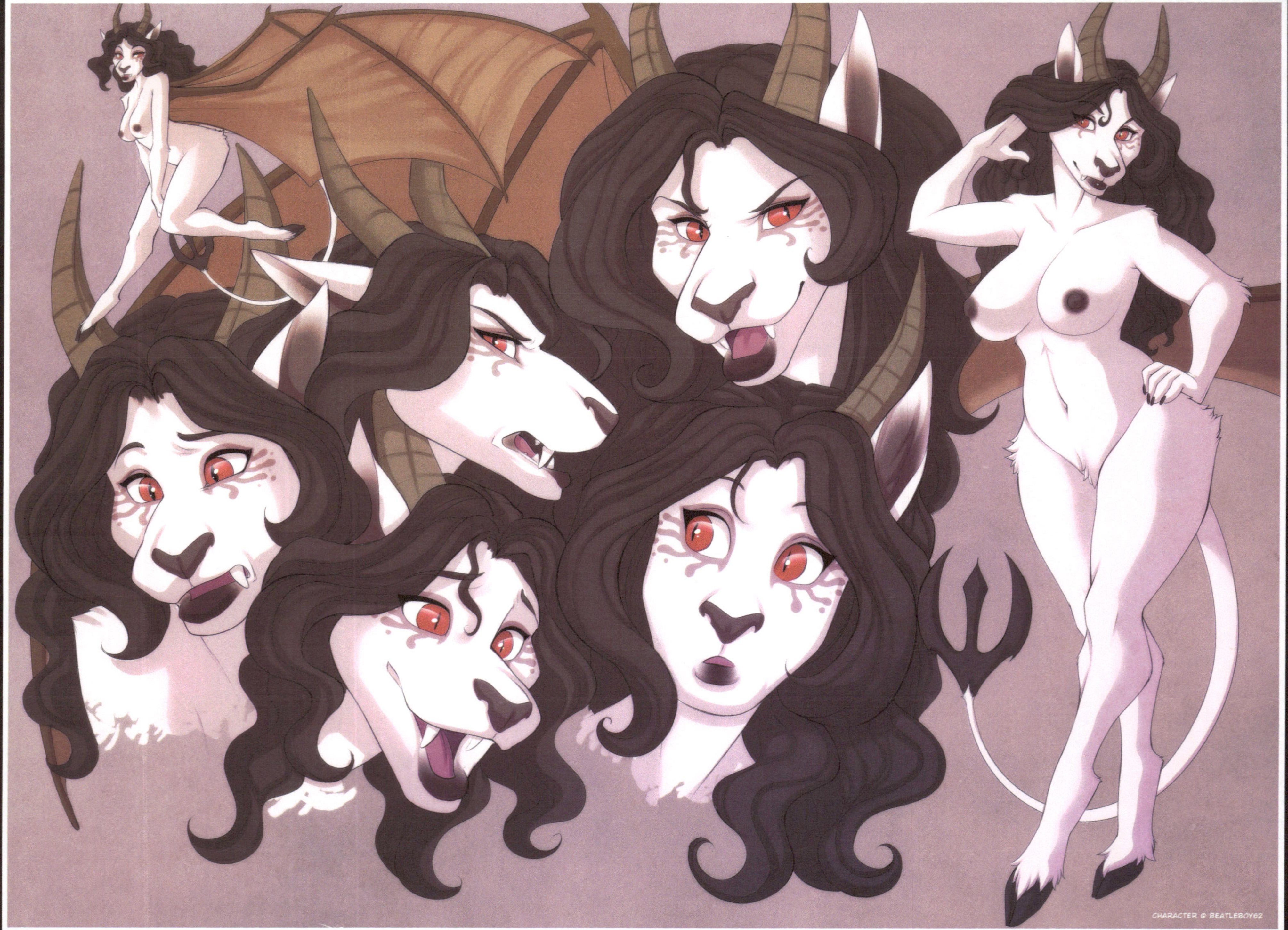
CHARACTER © BEATLEBOY62

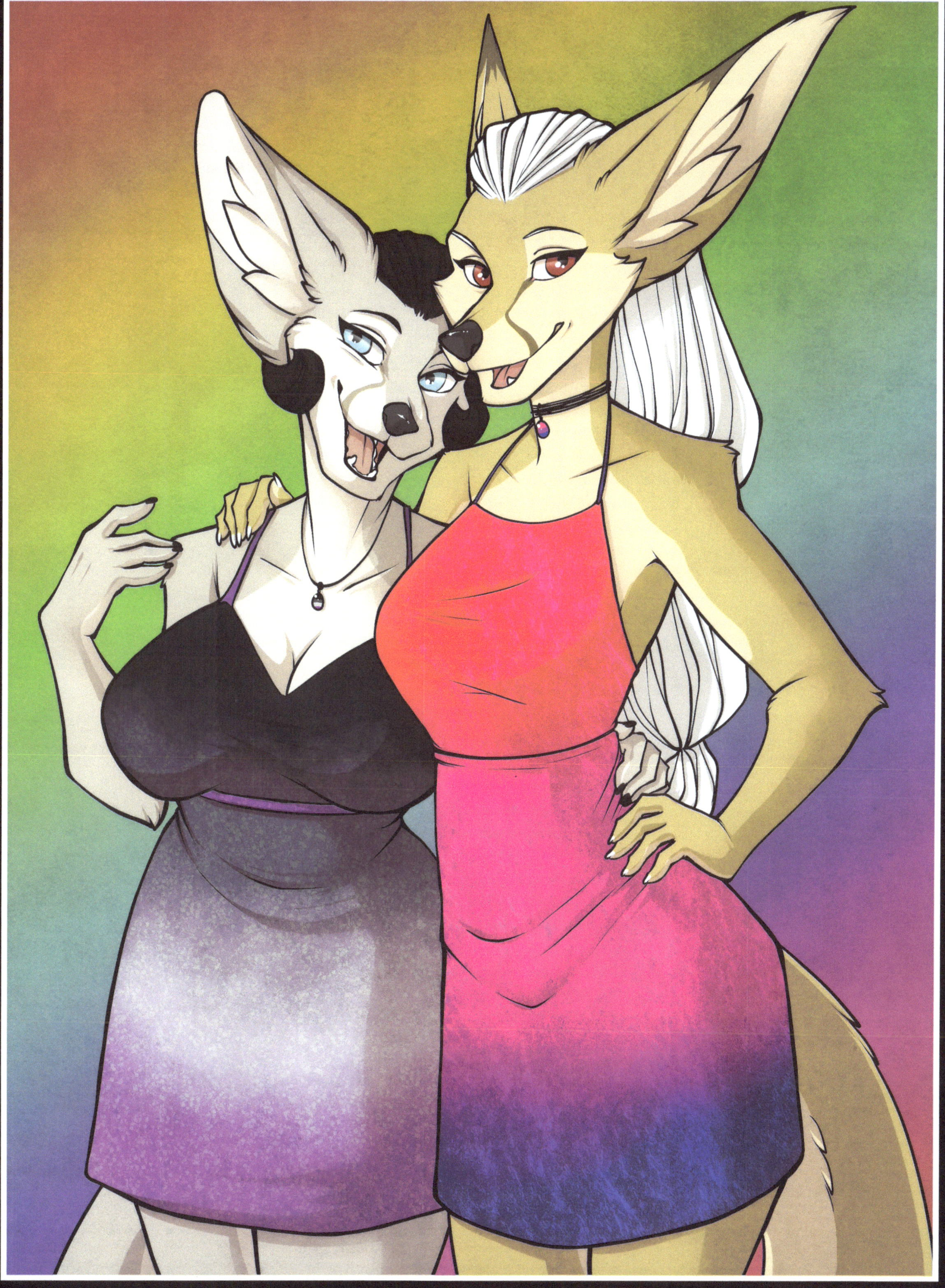

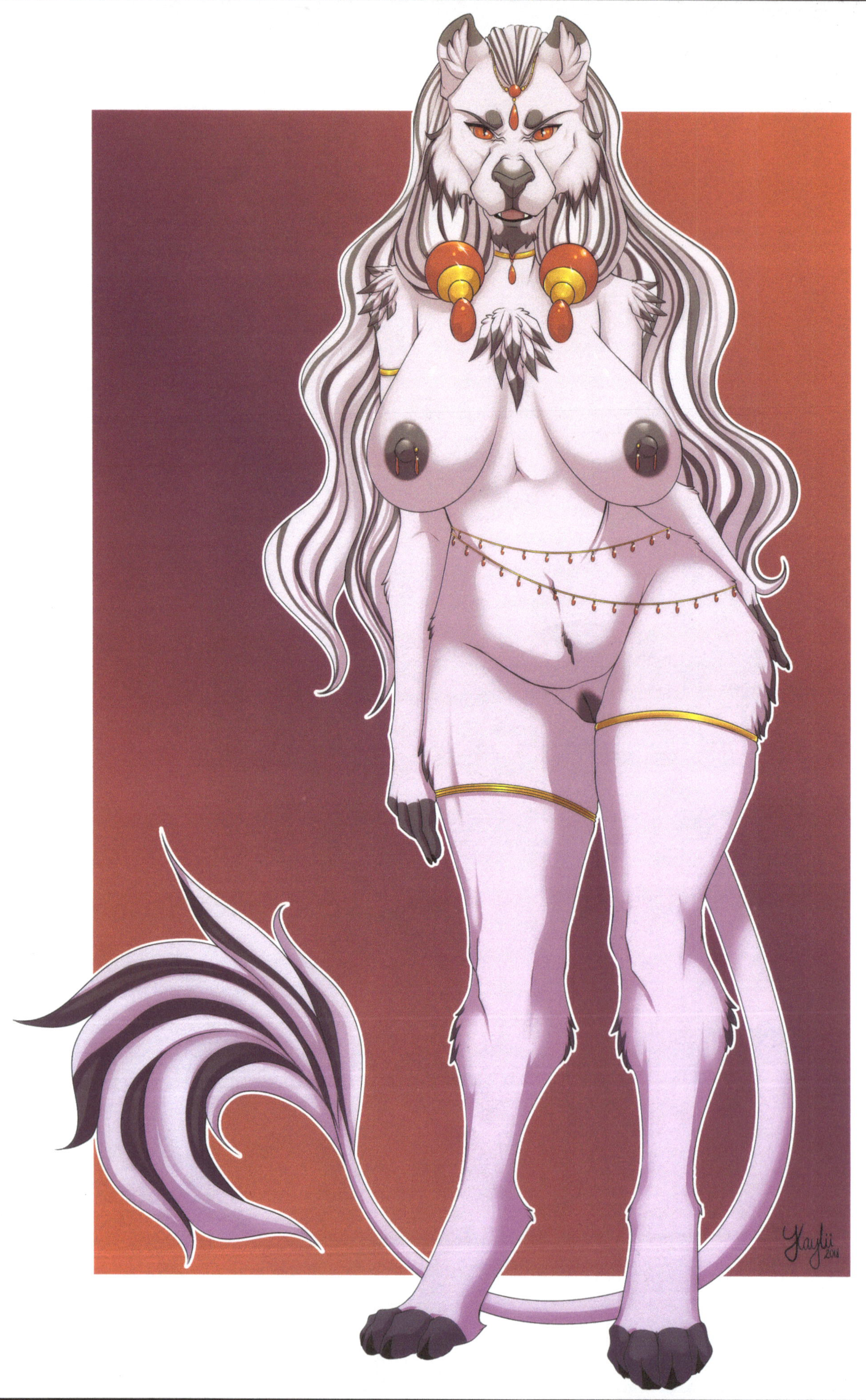
Kaylii
2016

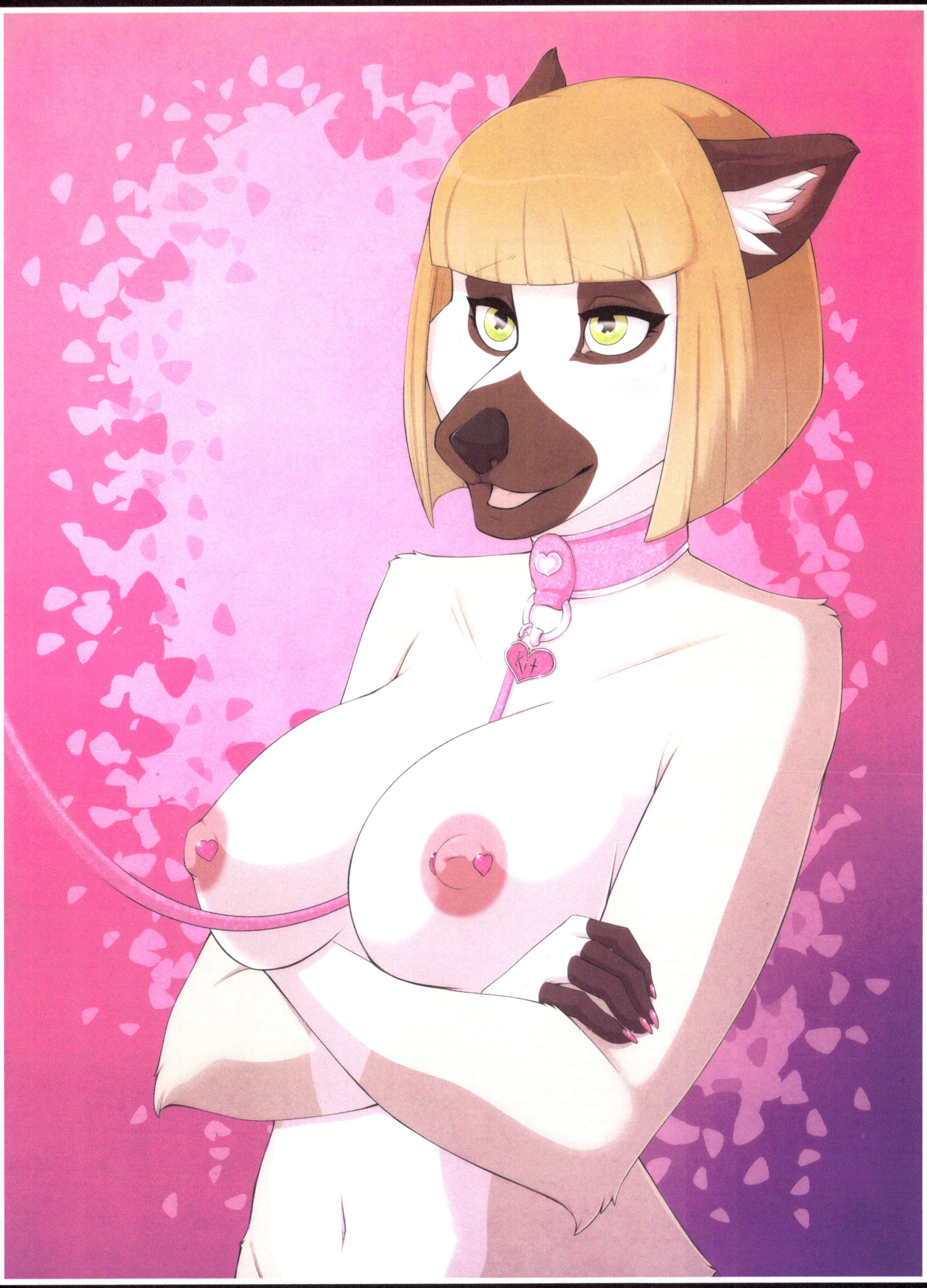
Kit

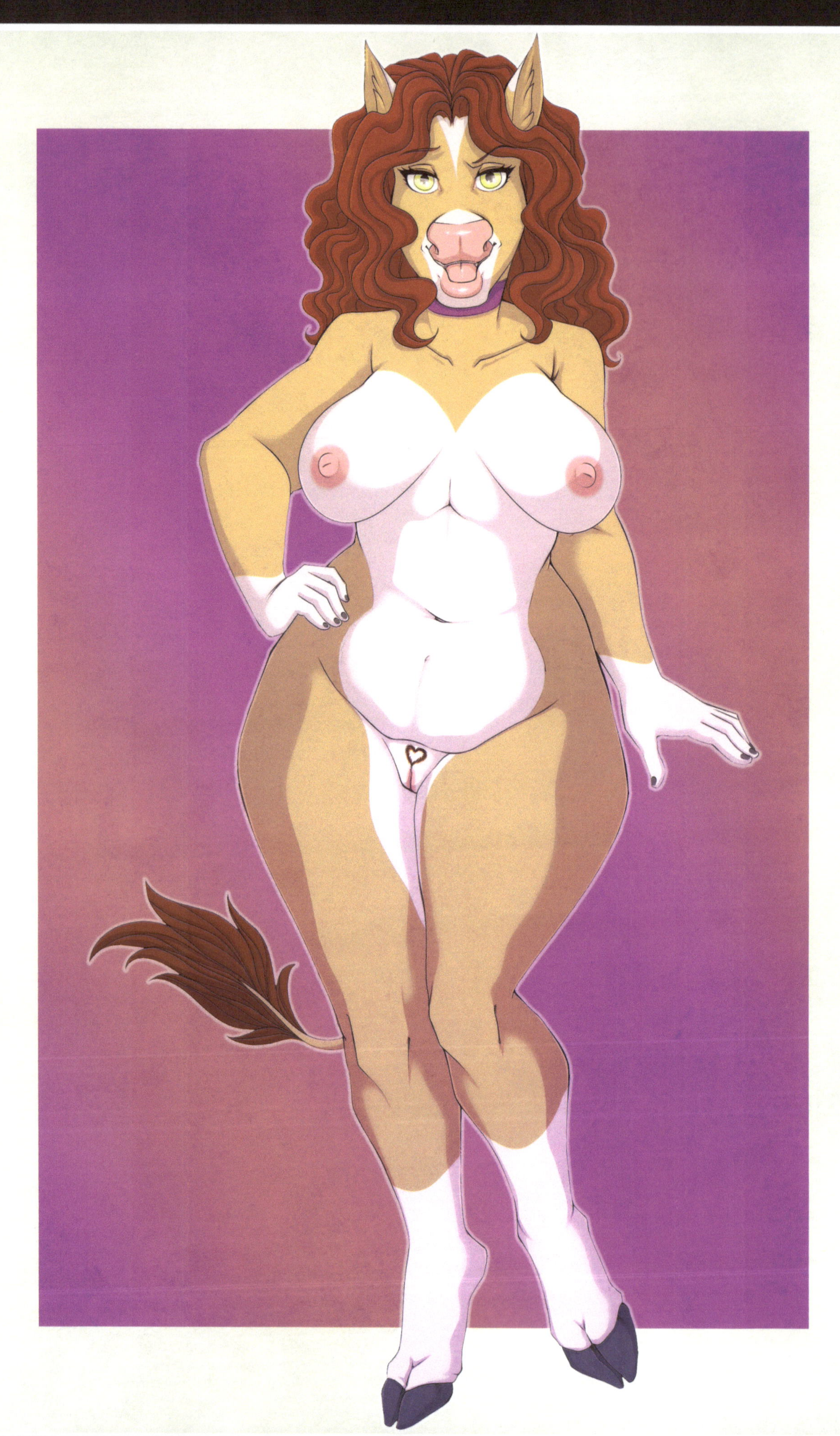

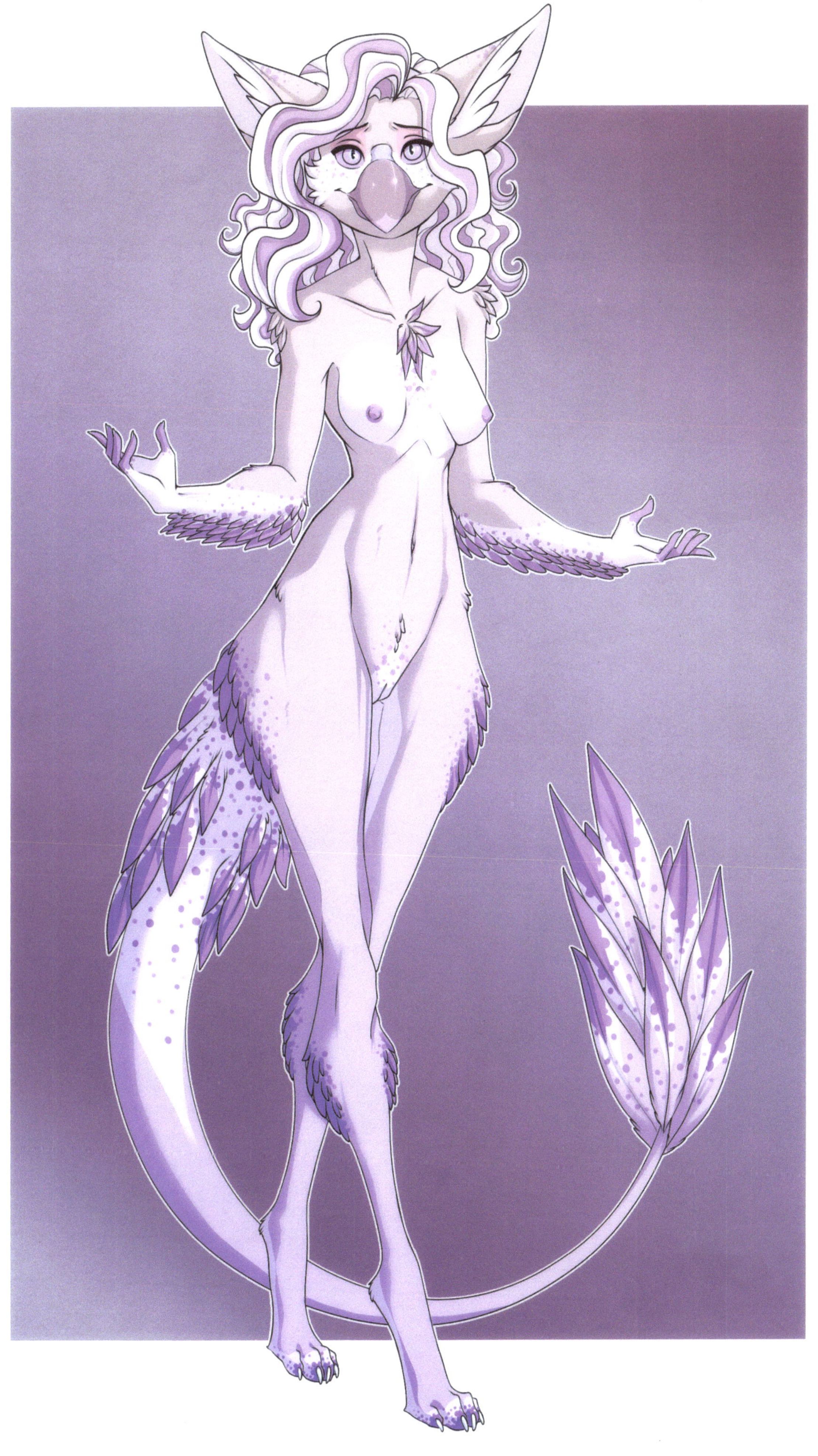

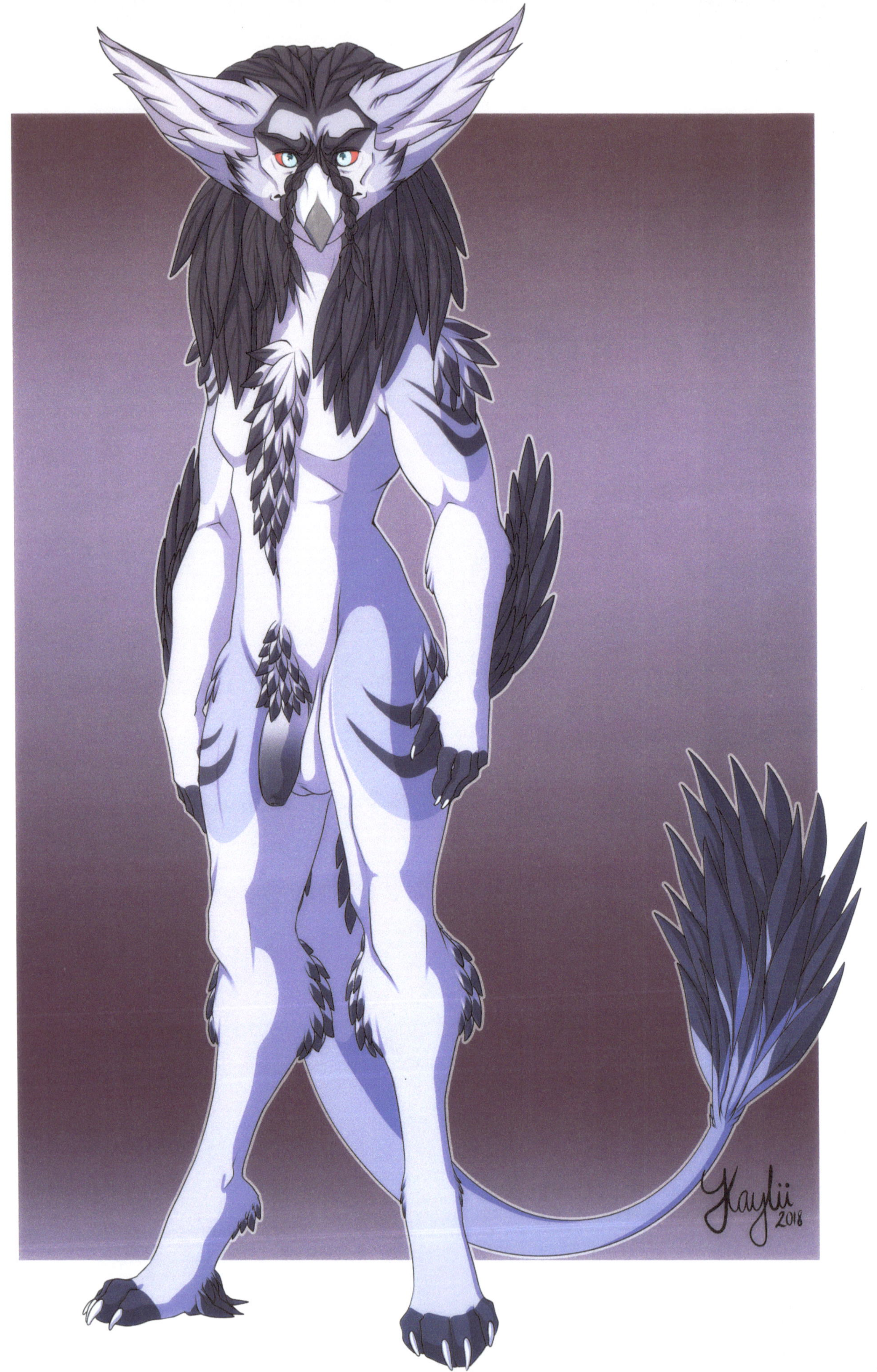
Kaylii
2018

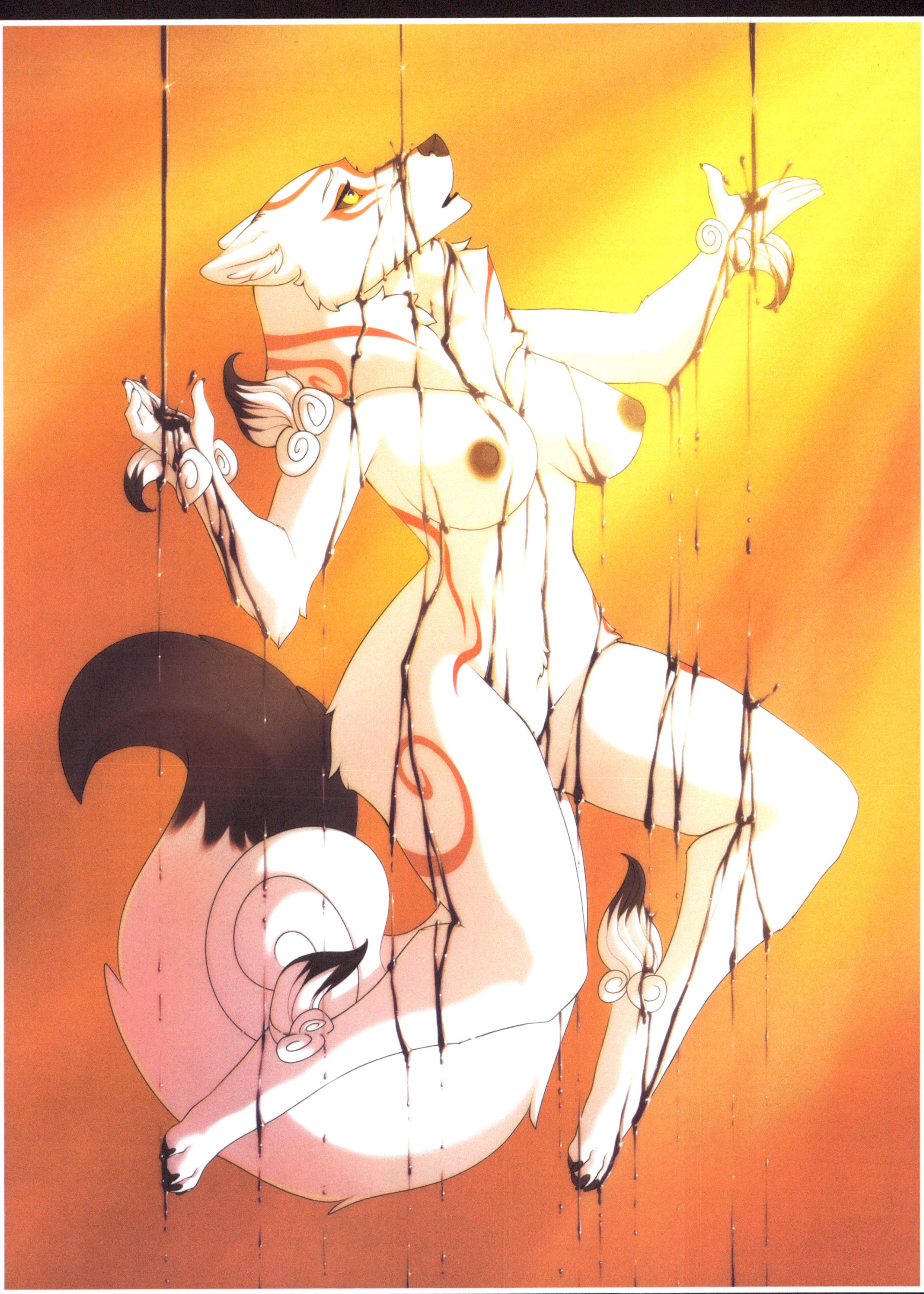

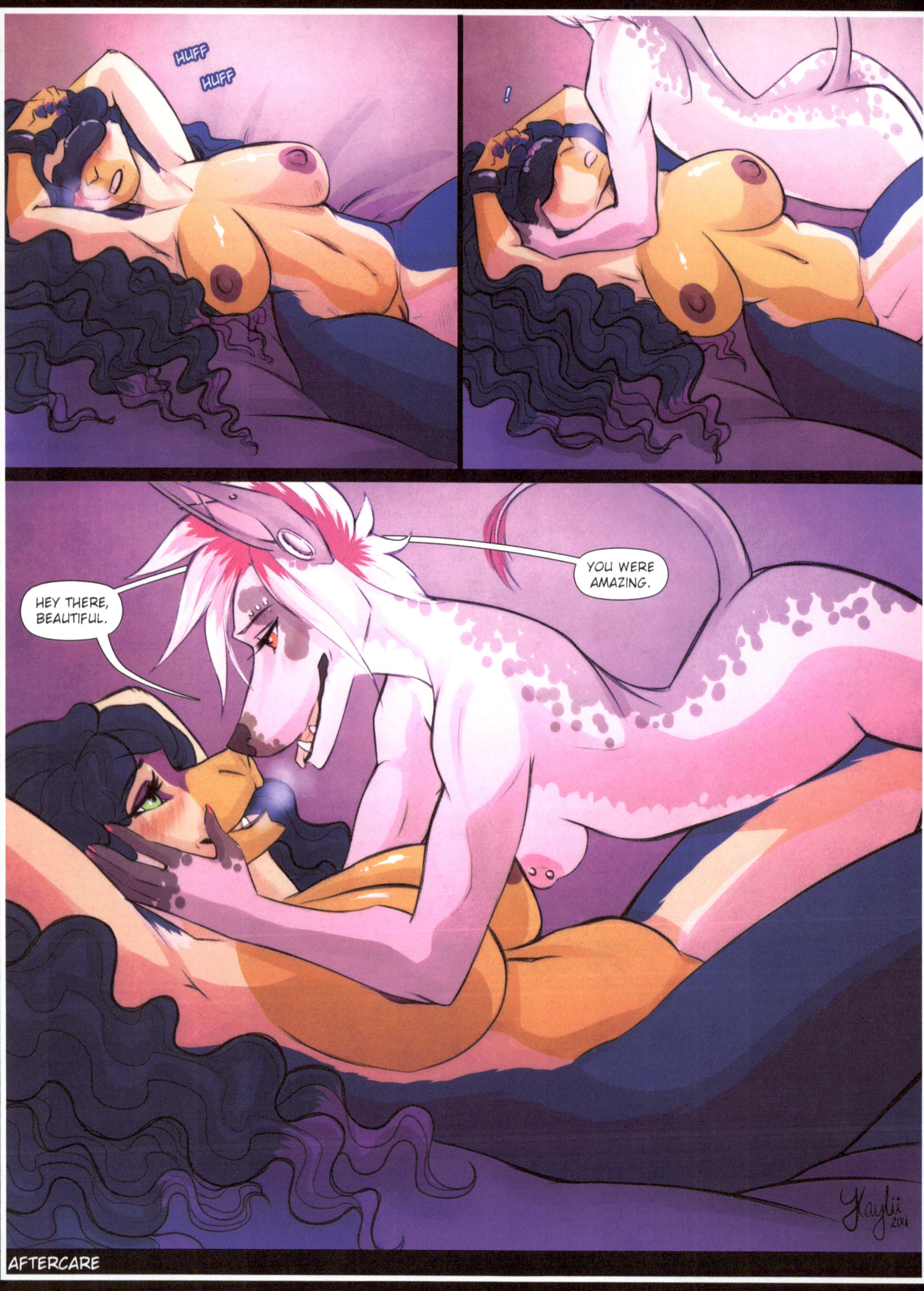
HUFF
HUFF
!
HEY THERE, BEAUTIFUL.
YOU WERE AMAZING.
Kaylii 2018
AFTERCARE

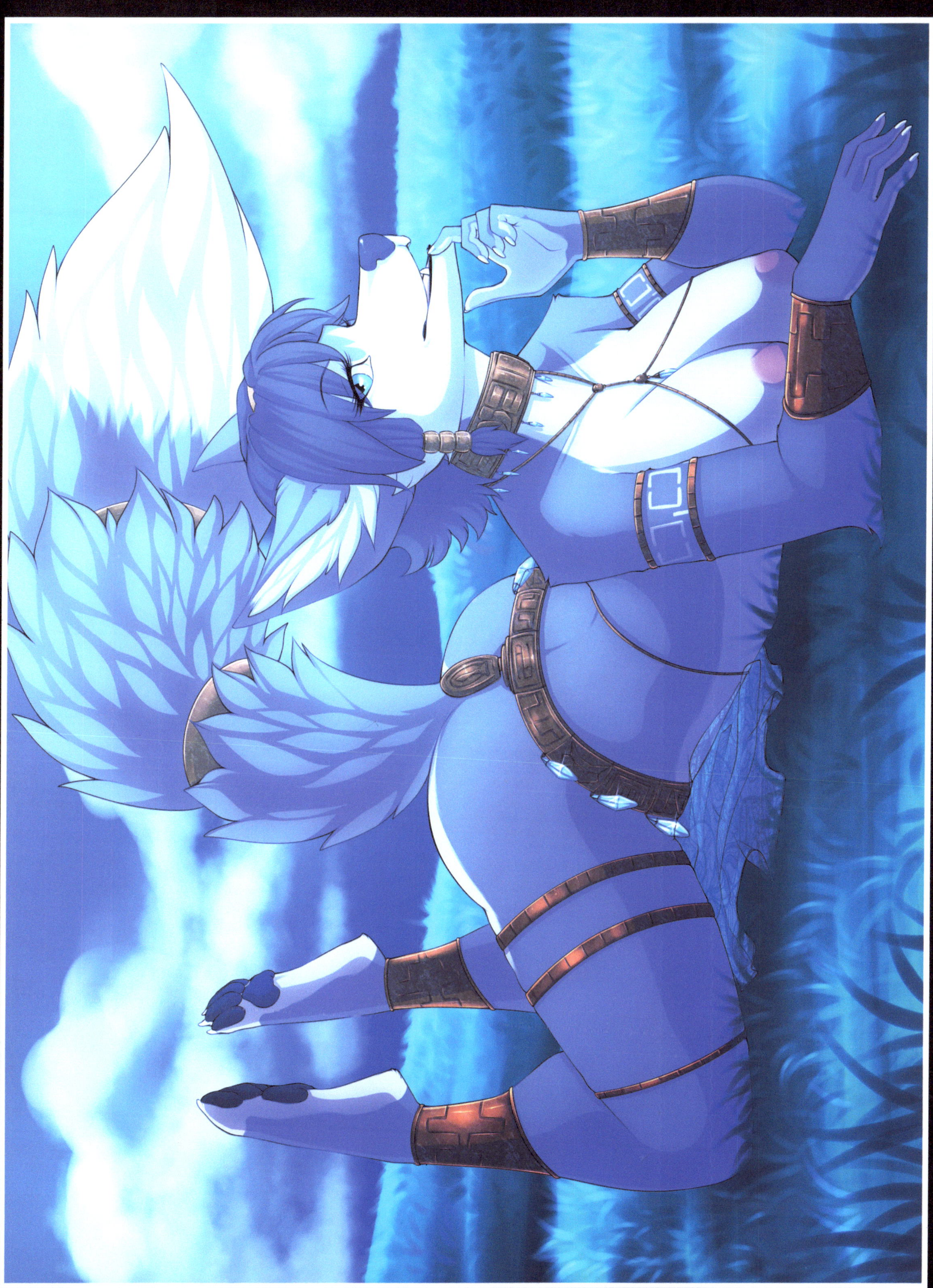

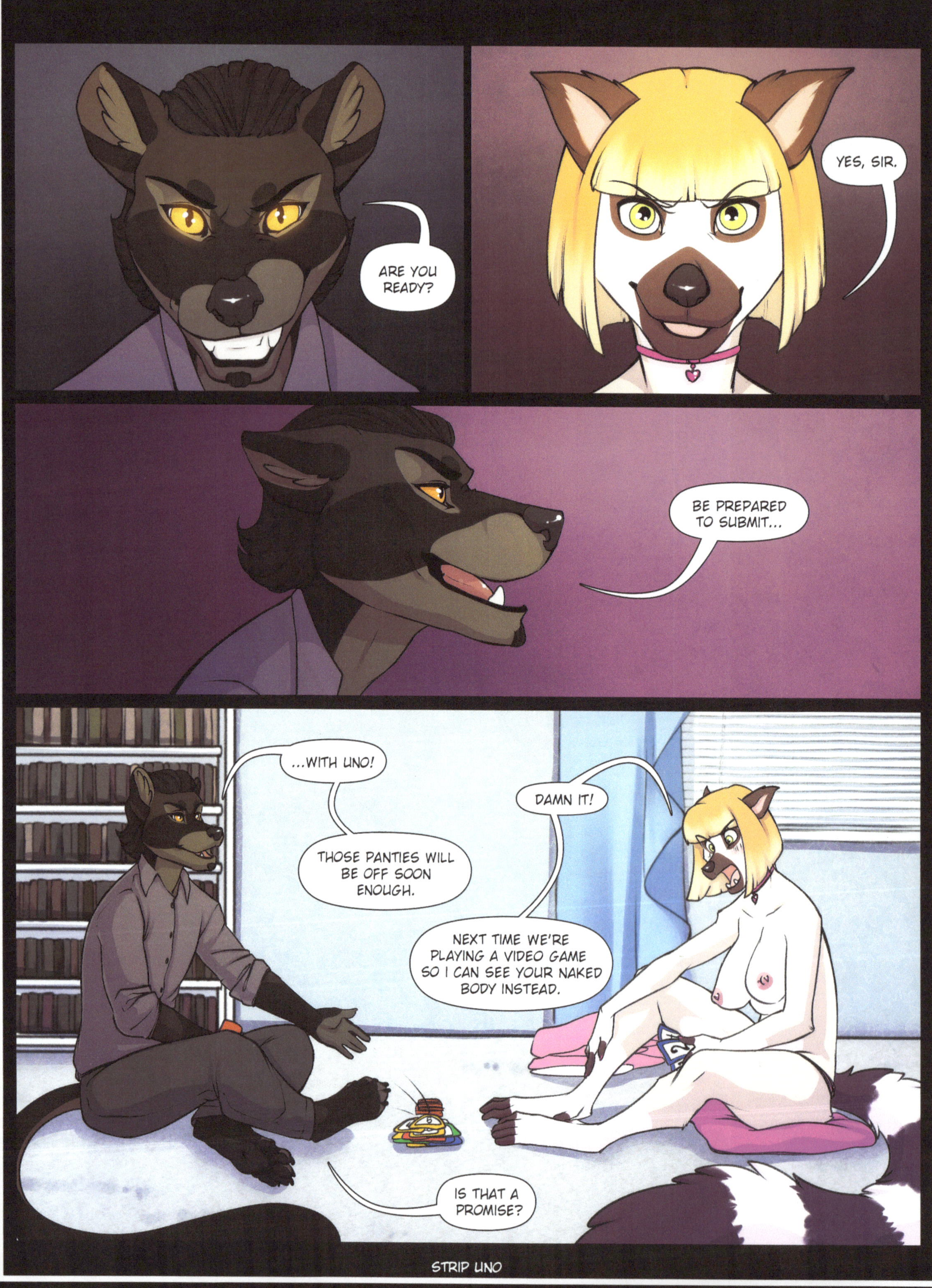
ARE YOU READY?
YES, SIR.
BE PREPARED TO SUBMIT...
...WITH UNO!
THOSE PANTIES WILL BE OFF SOON ENOUGH.
DAMN IT!
NEXT TIME WE'RE PLAYING A VIDEO GAME SO I CAN SEE YOUR NAKED BODY INSTEAD.
IS THAT A PROMISE?

STRIP UNO

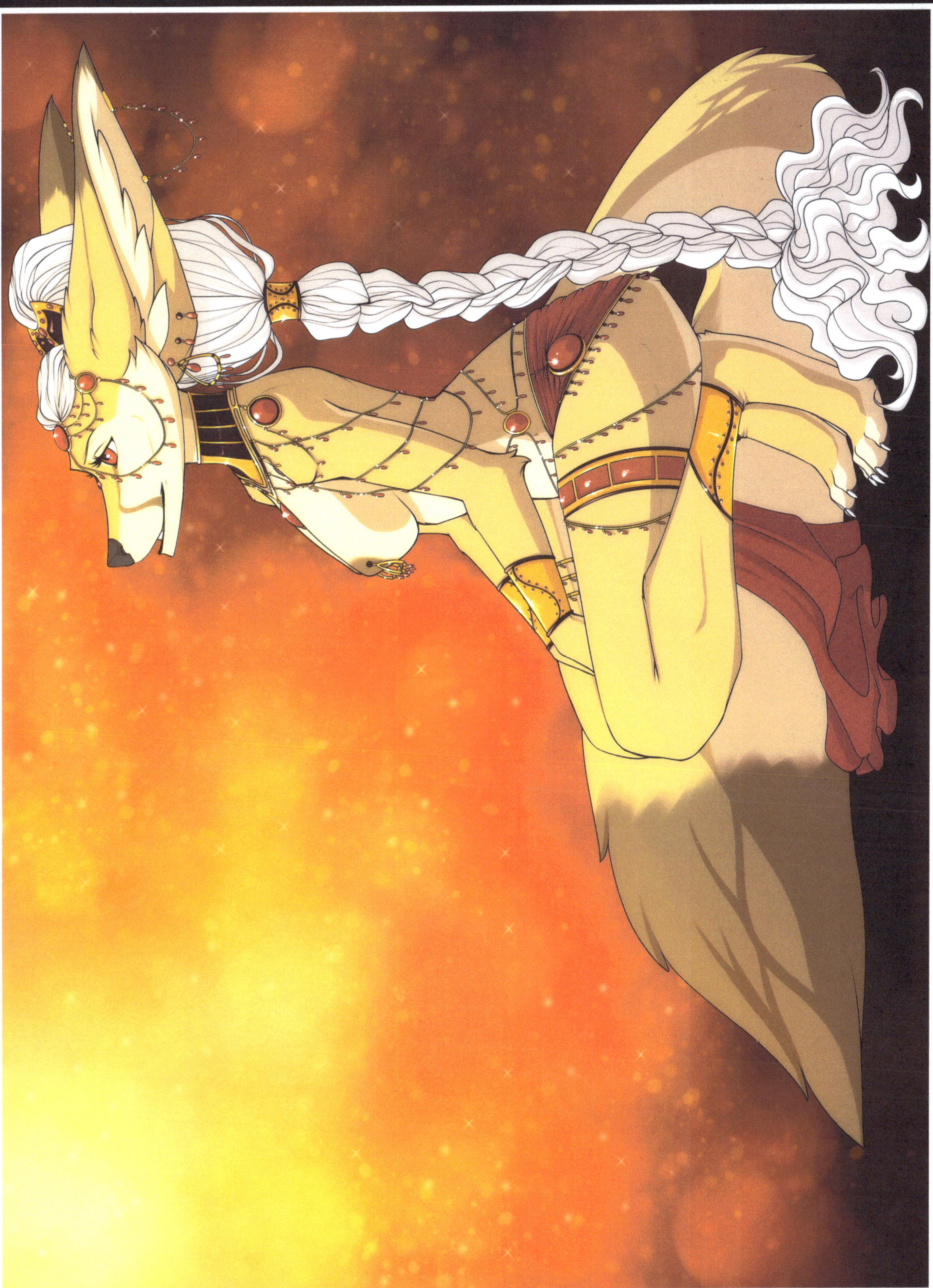

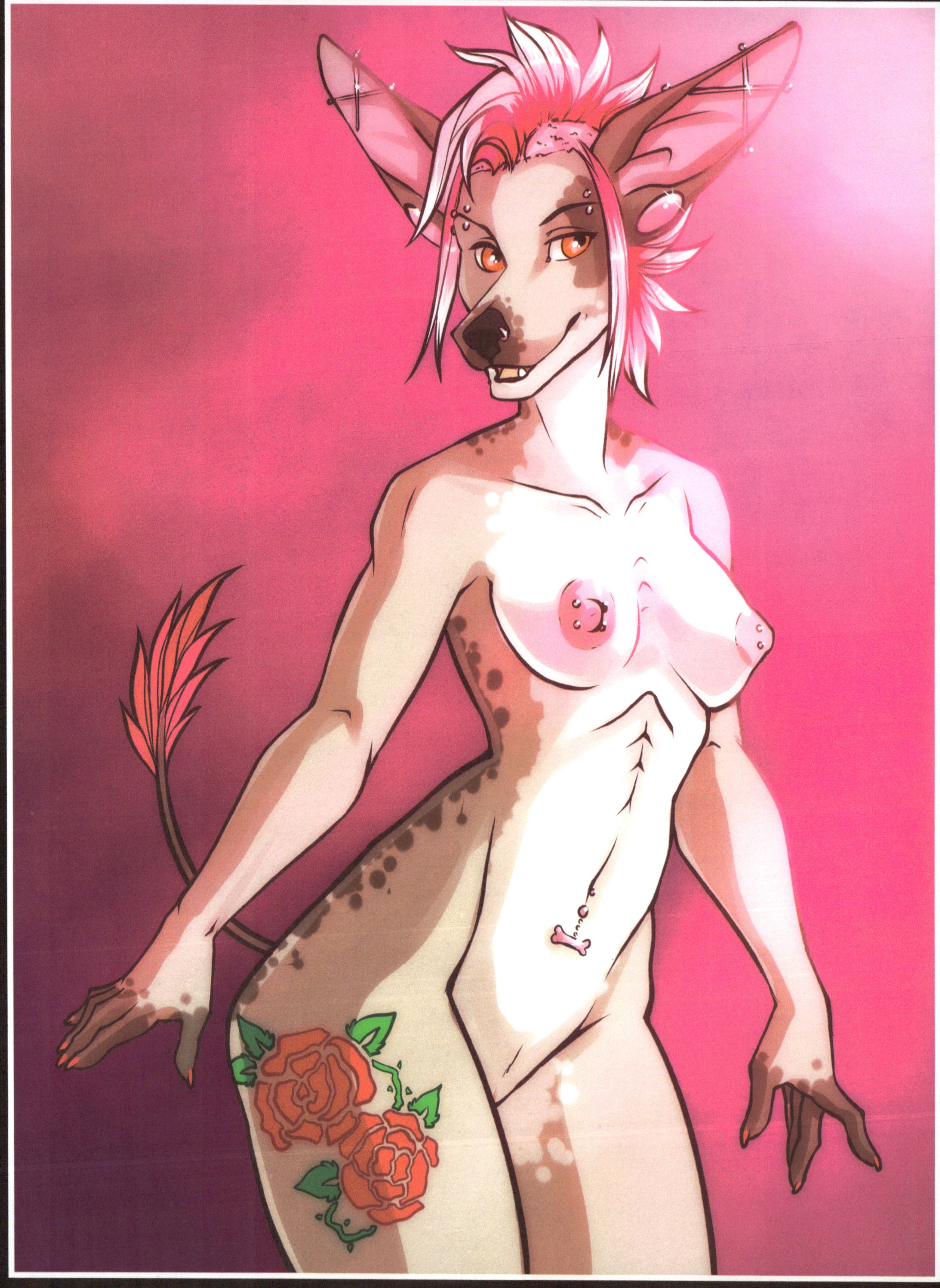

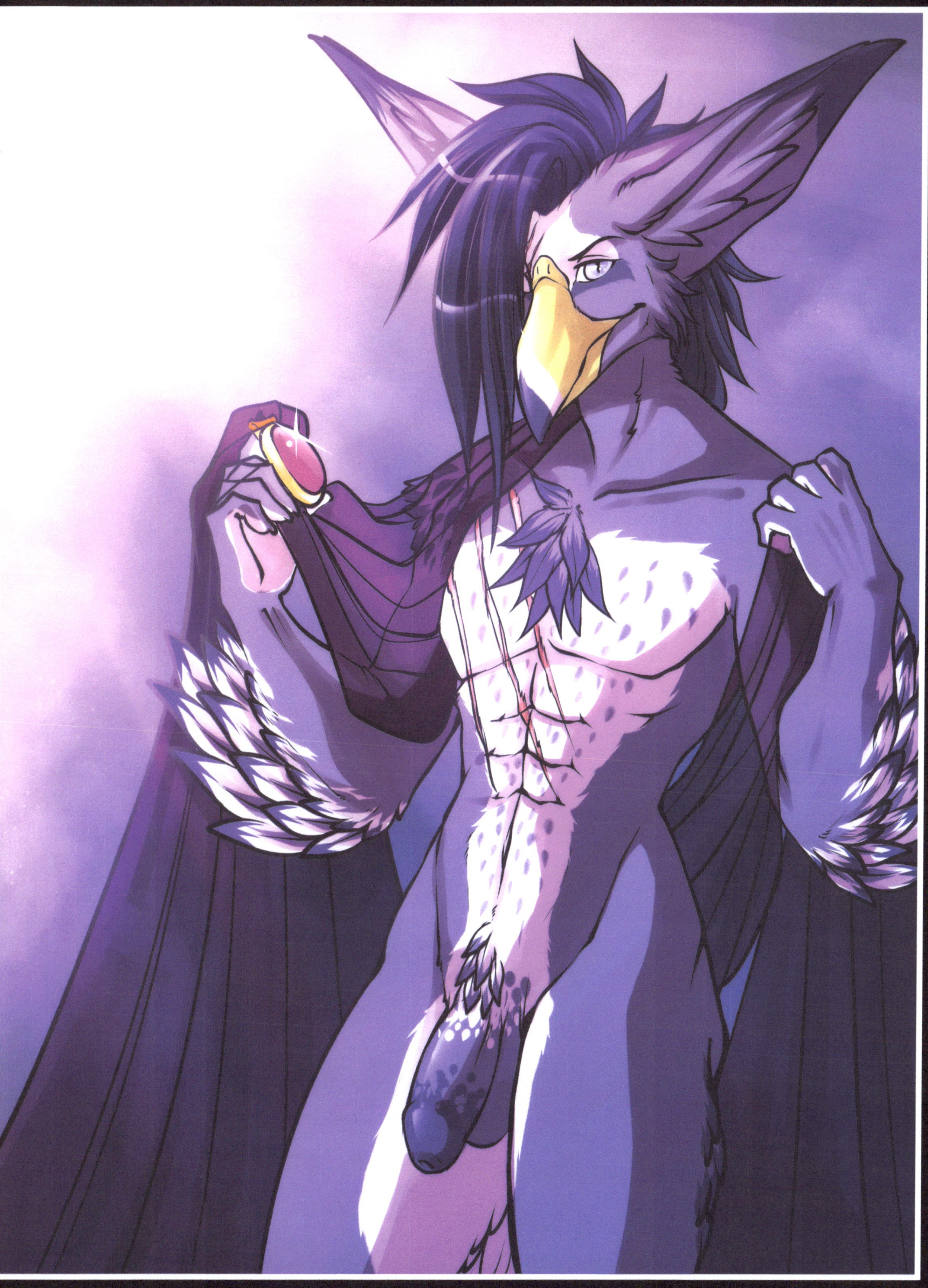

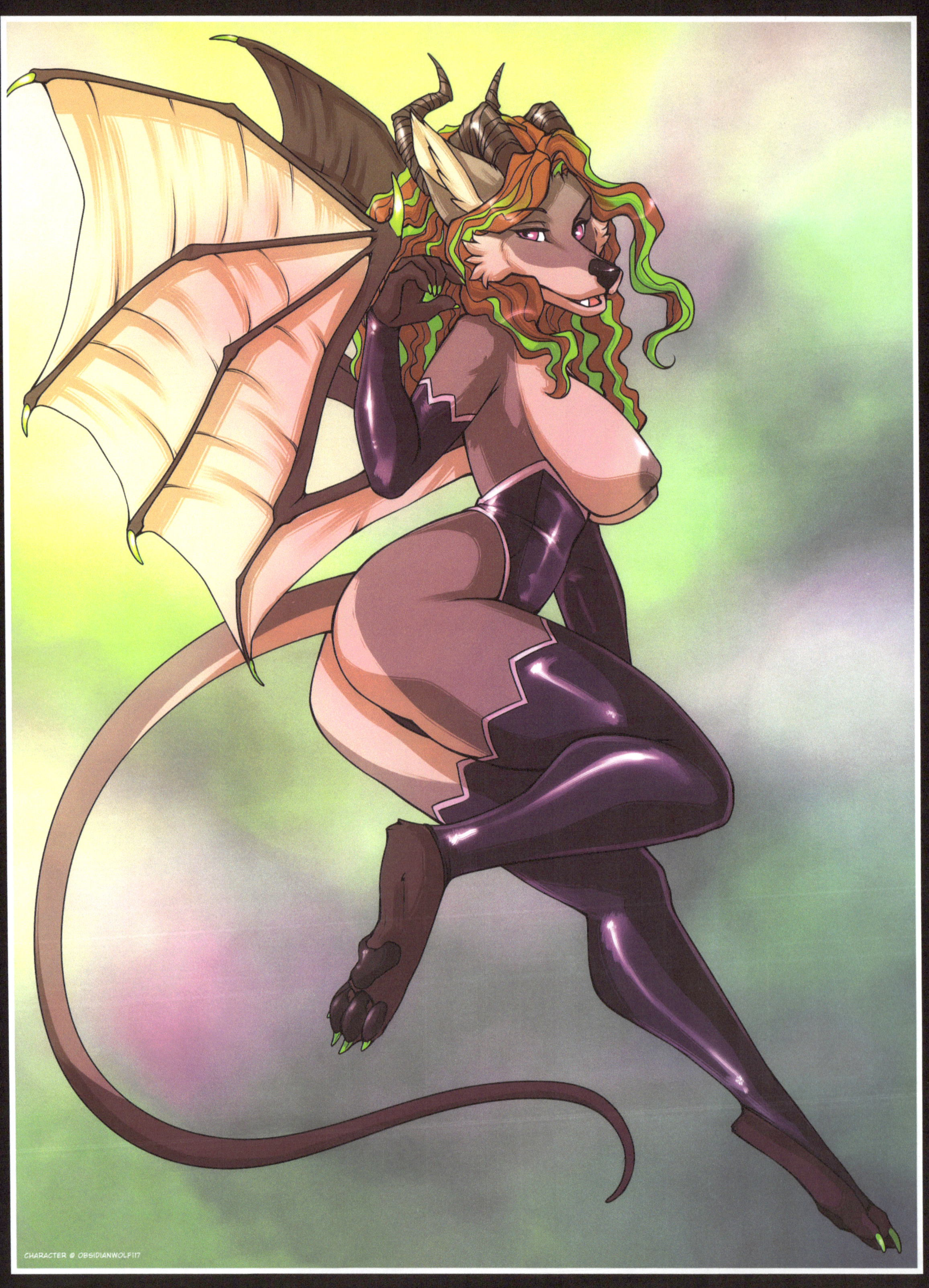
CHARACTER @ OBSIDIANWOLF117

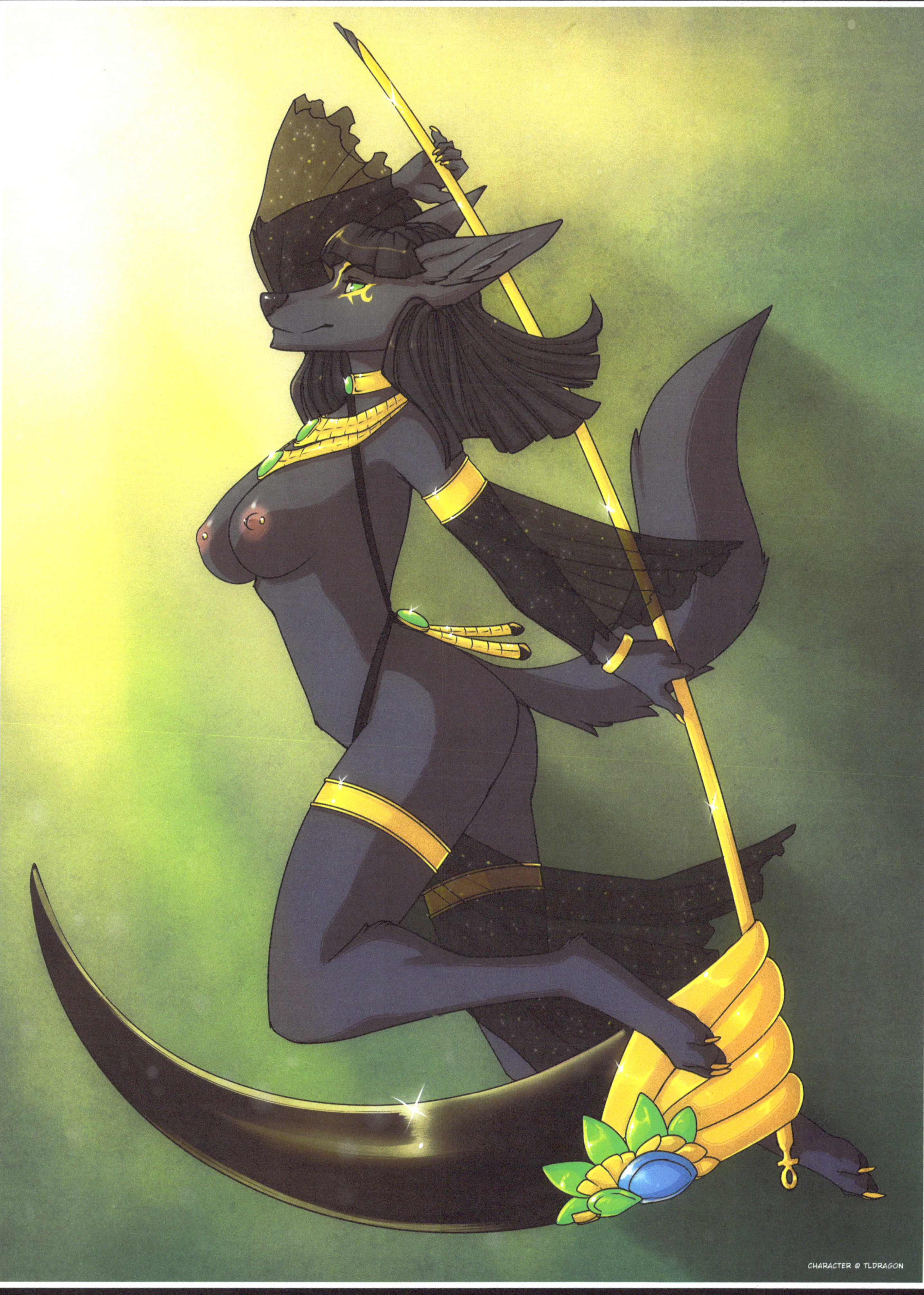
CHARACTER © TLDRAGON

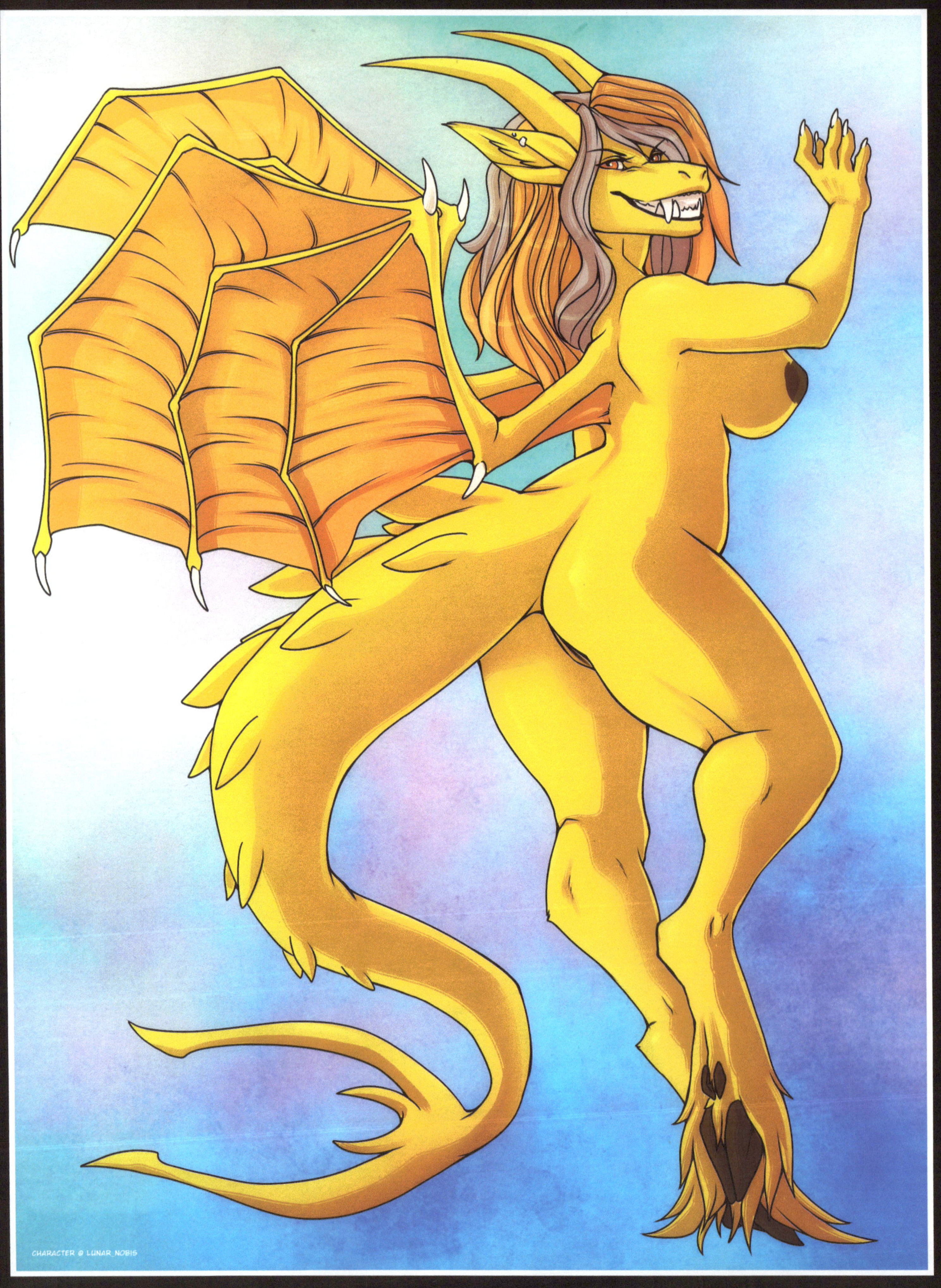
CHARACTER © LUNAR_NOBIS

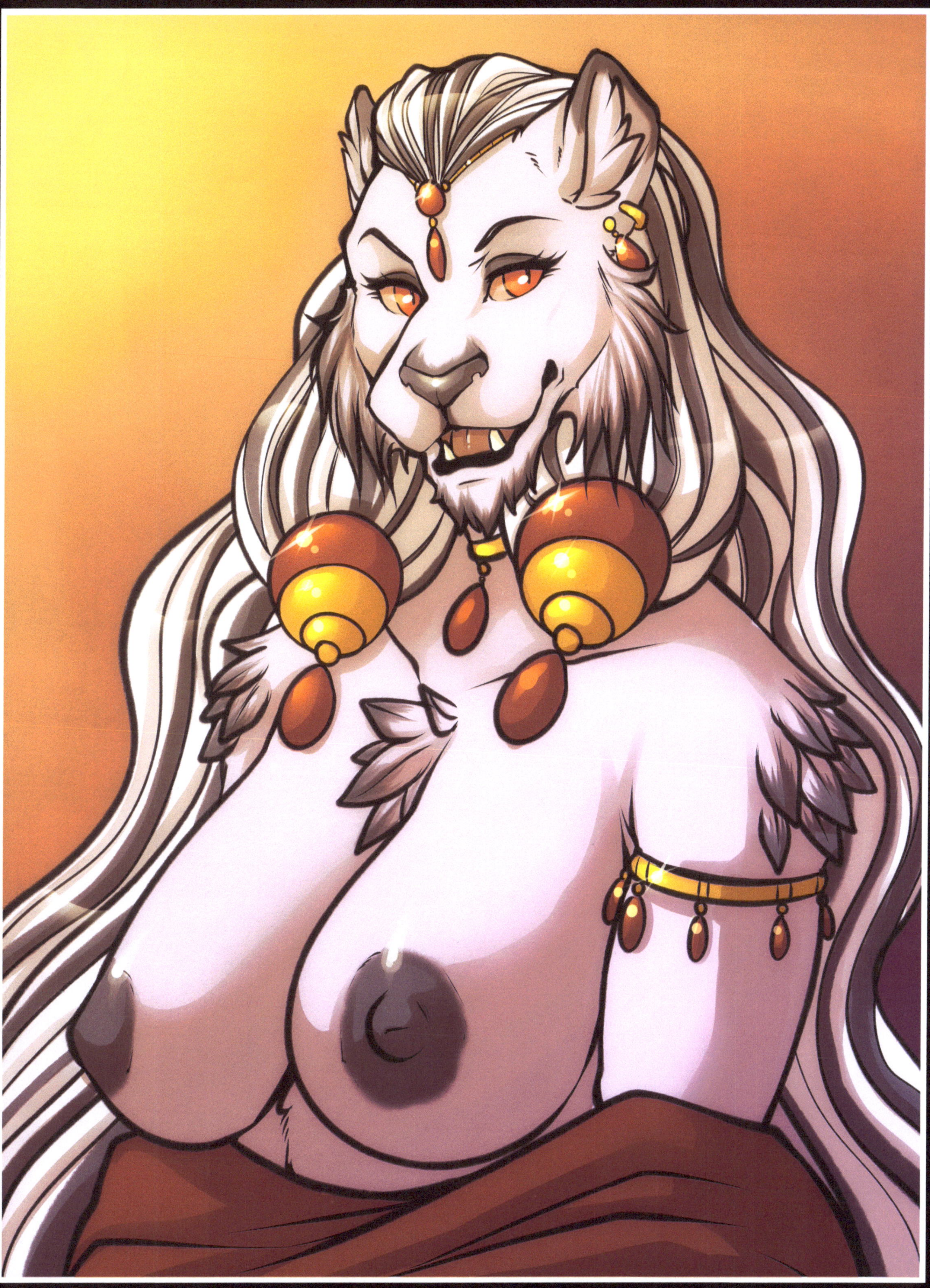

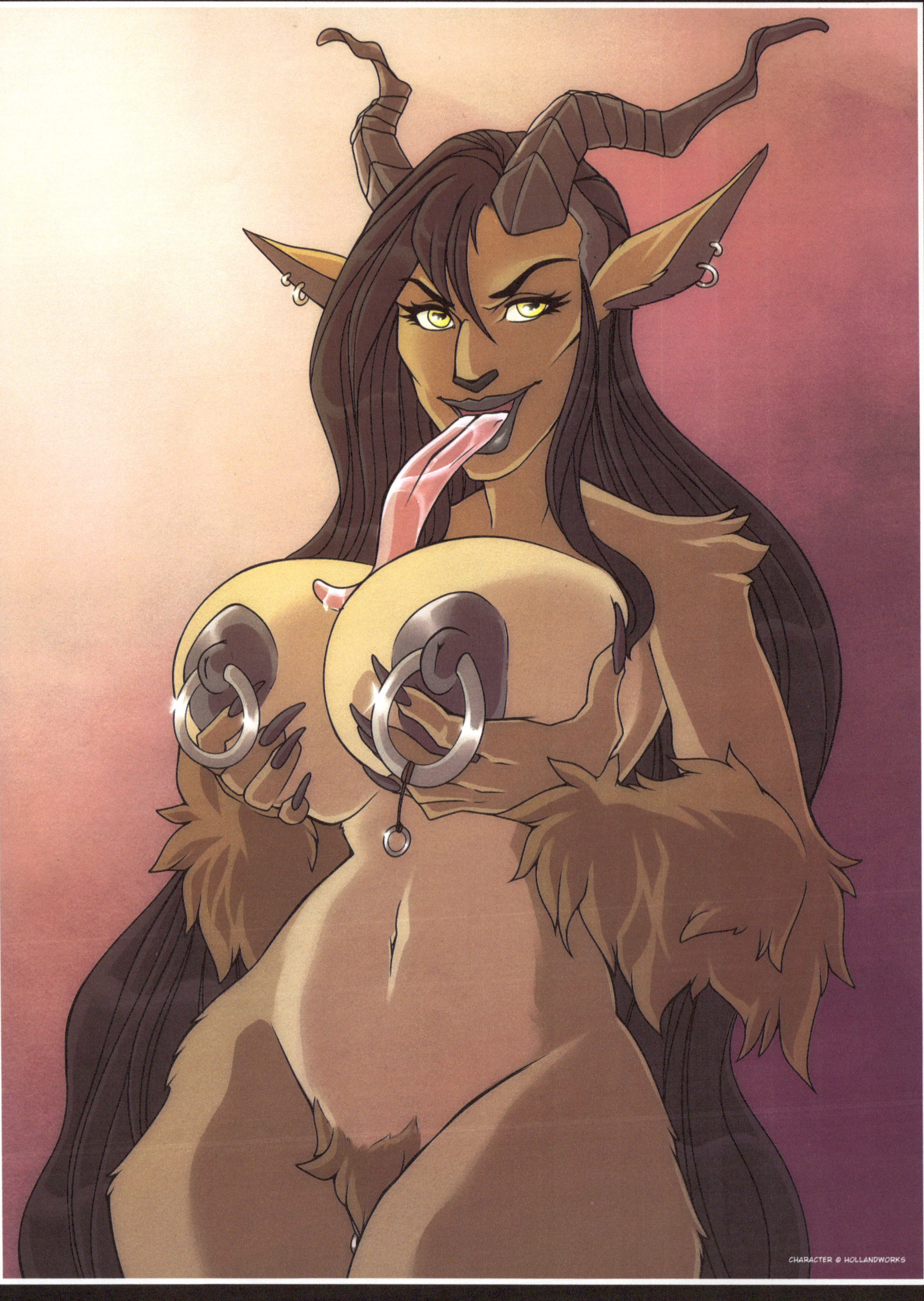

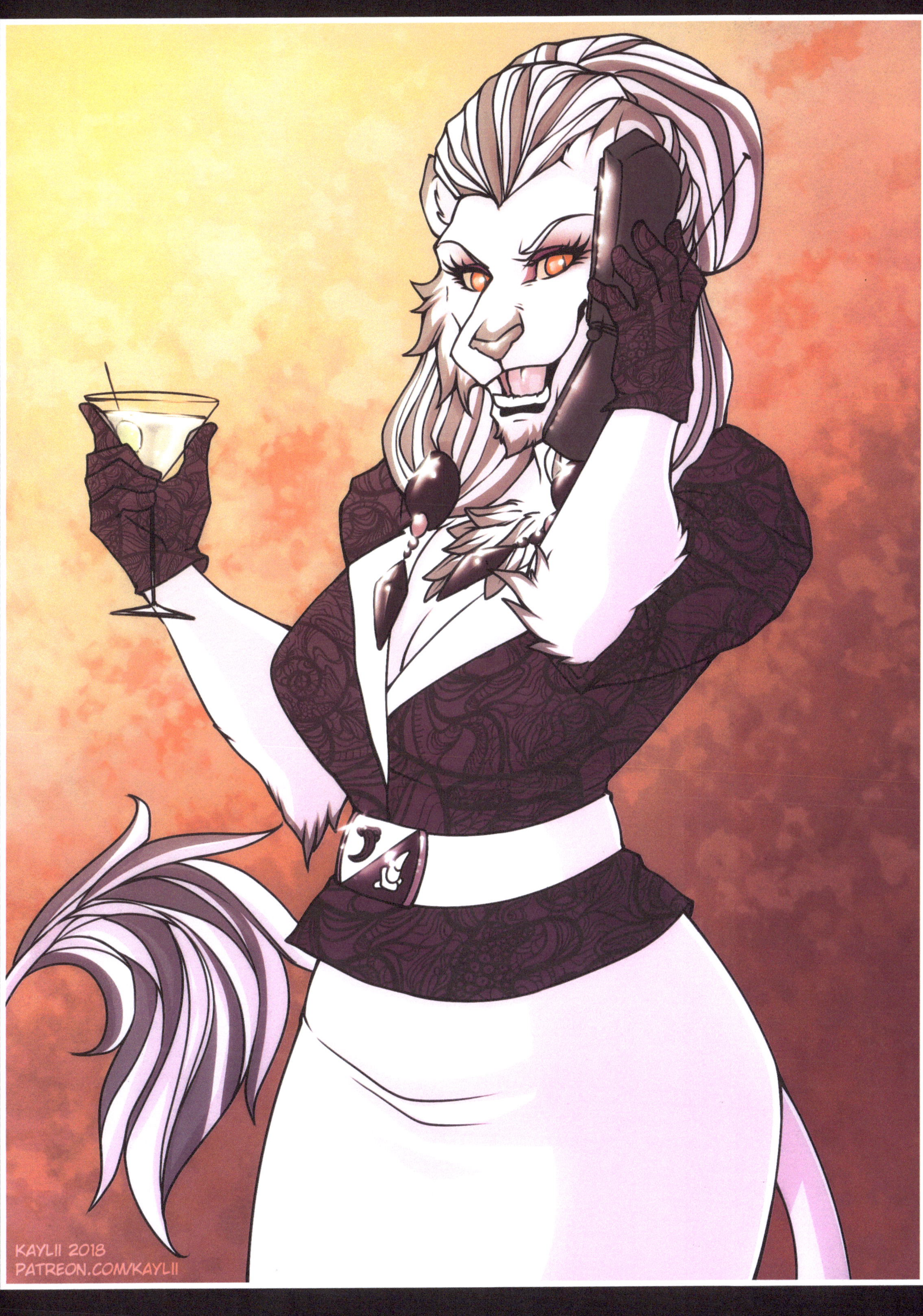
KAYLII 2018
PATREON.COM/KAYLII

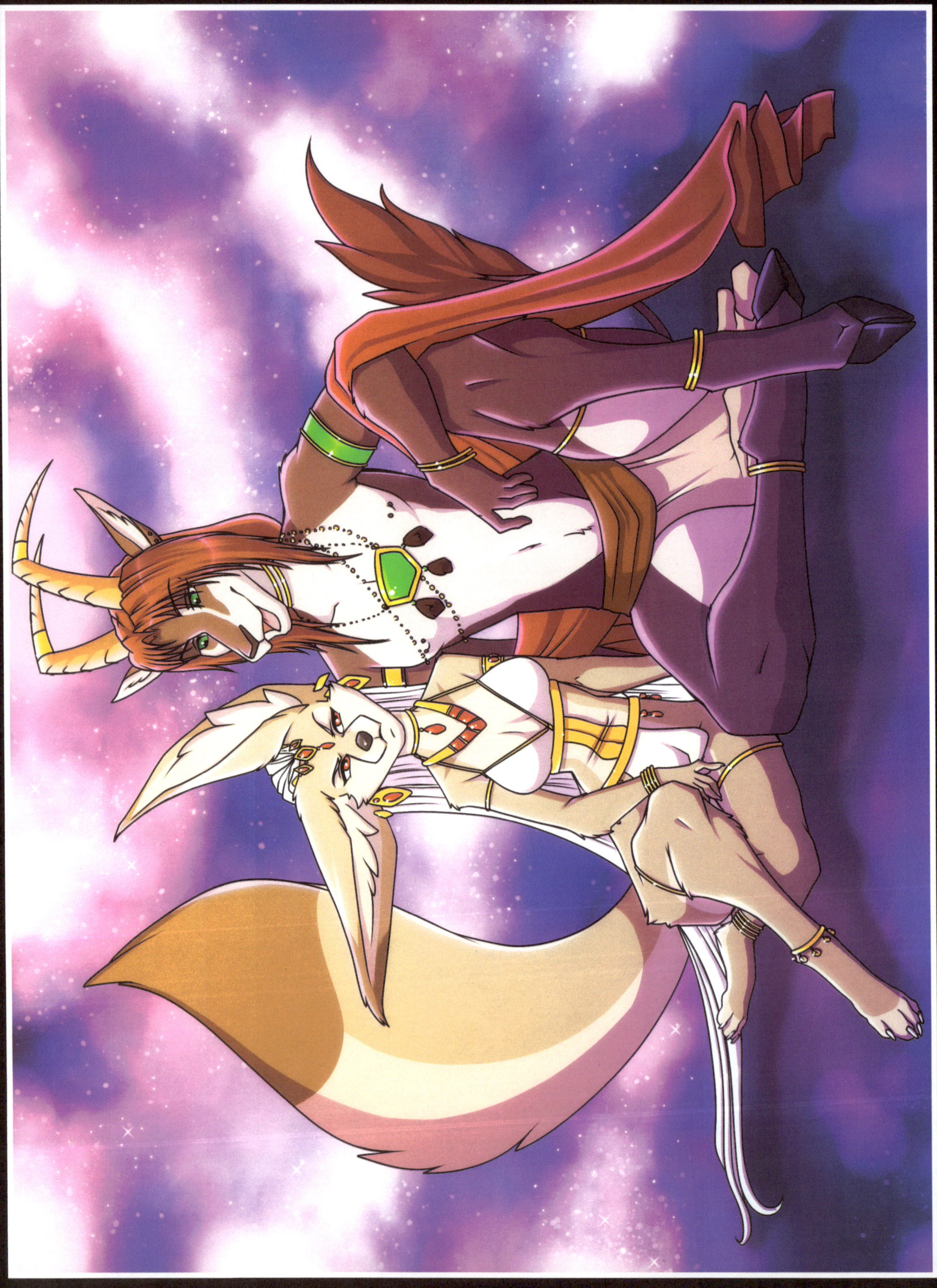

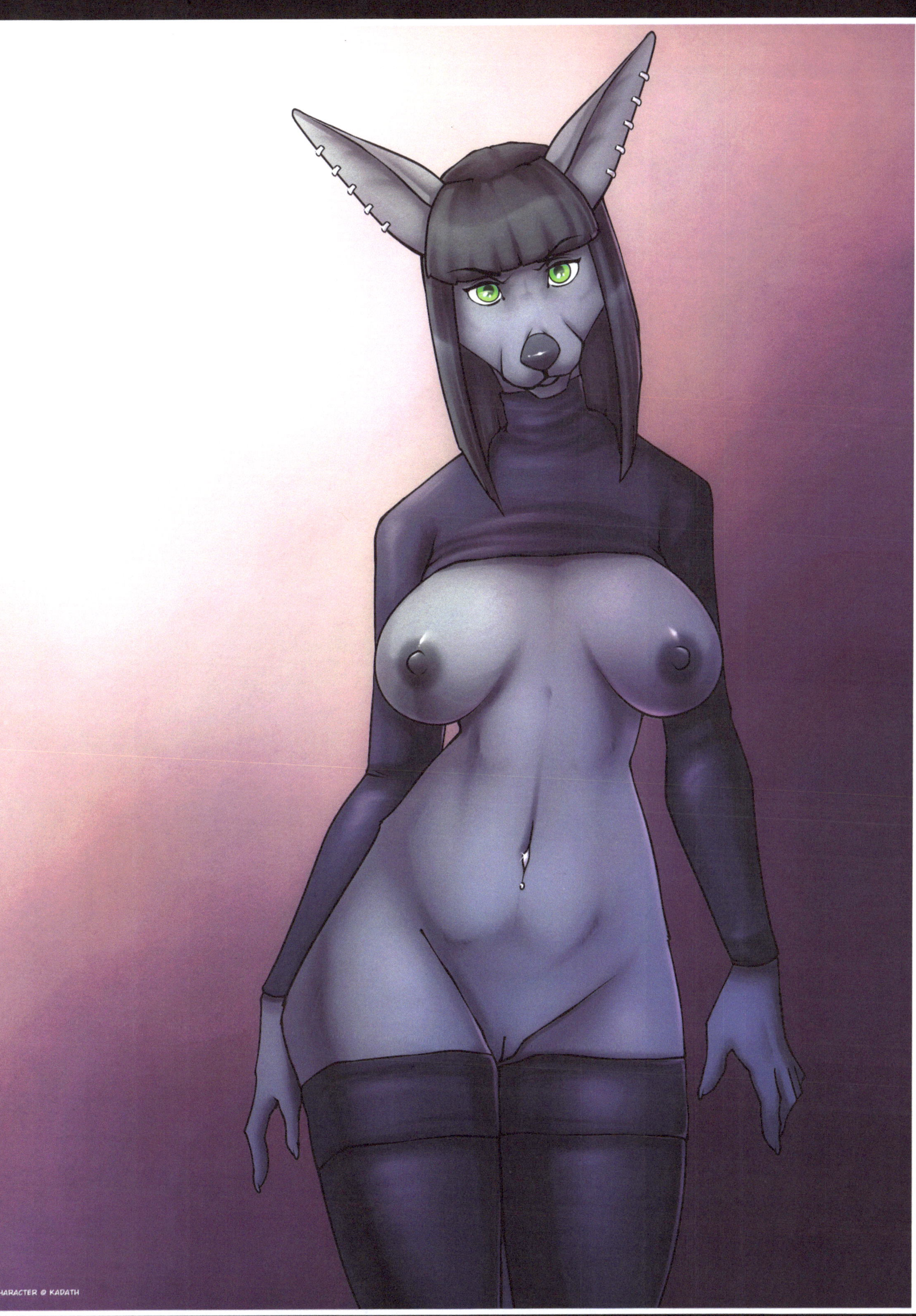
CHARACTER © KADATH

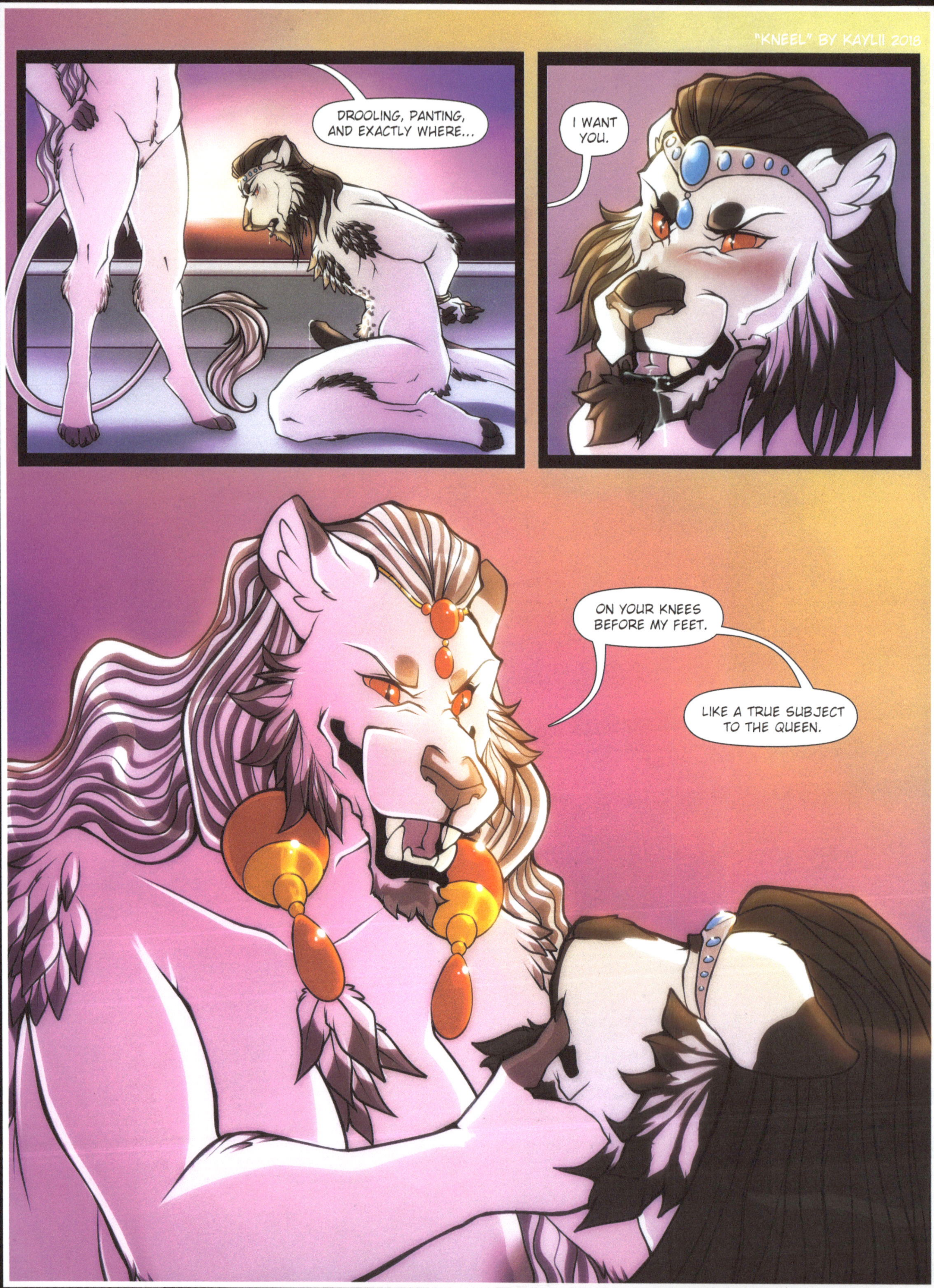

"KNEEL" BY KAYLII 2018

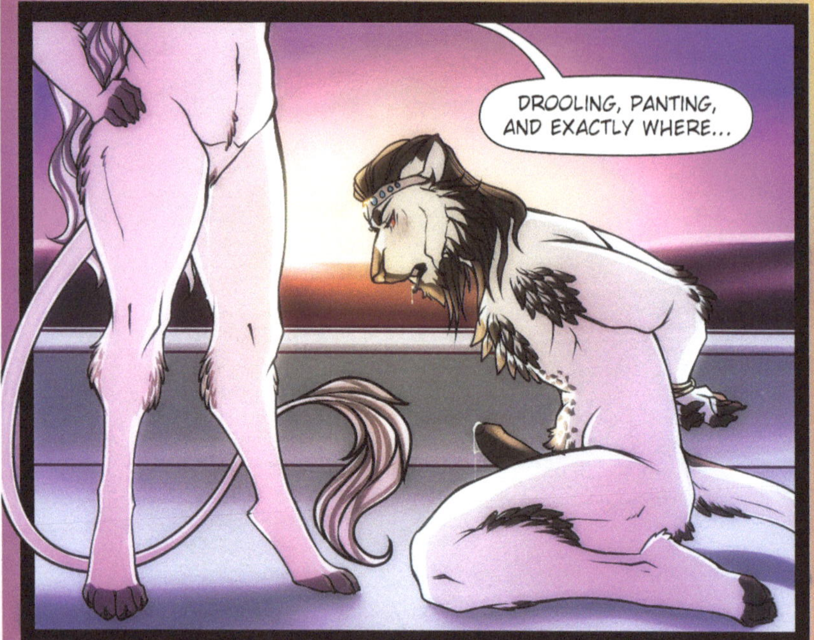

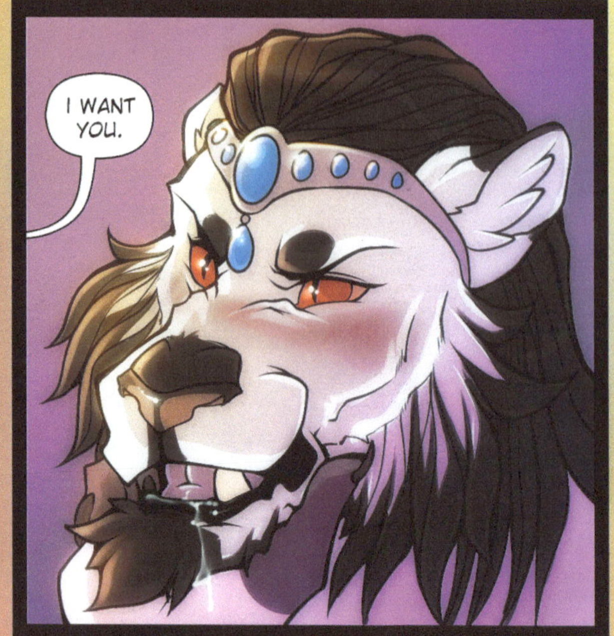

ON YOUR KNEES BEFORE MY FEET.

LIKE A TRUE SUBJECT TO THE QUEEN.

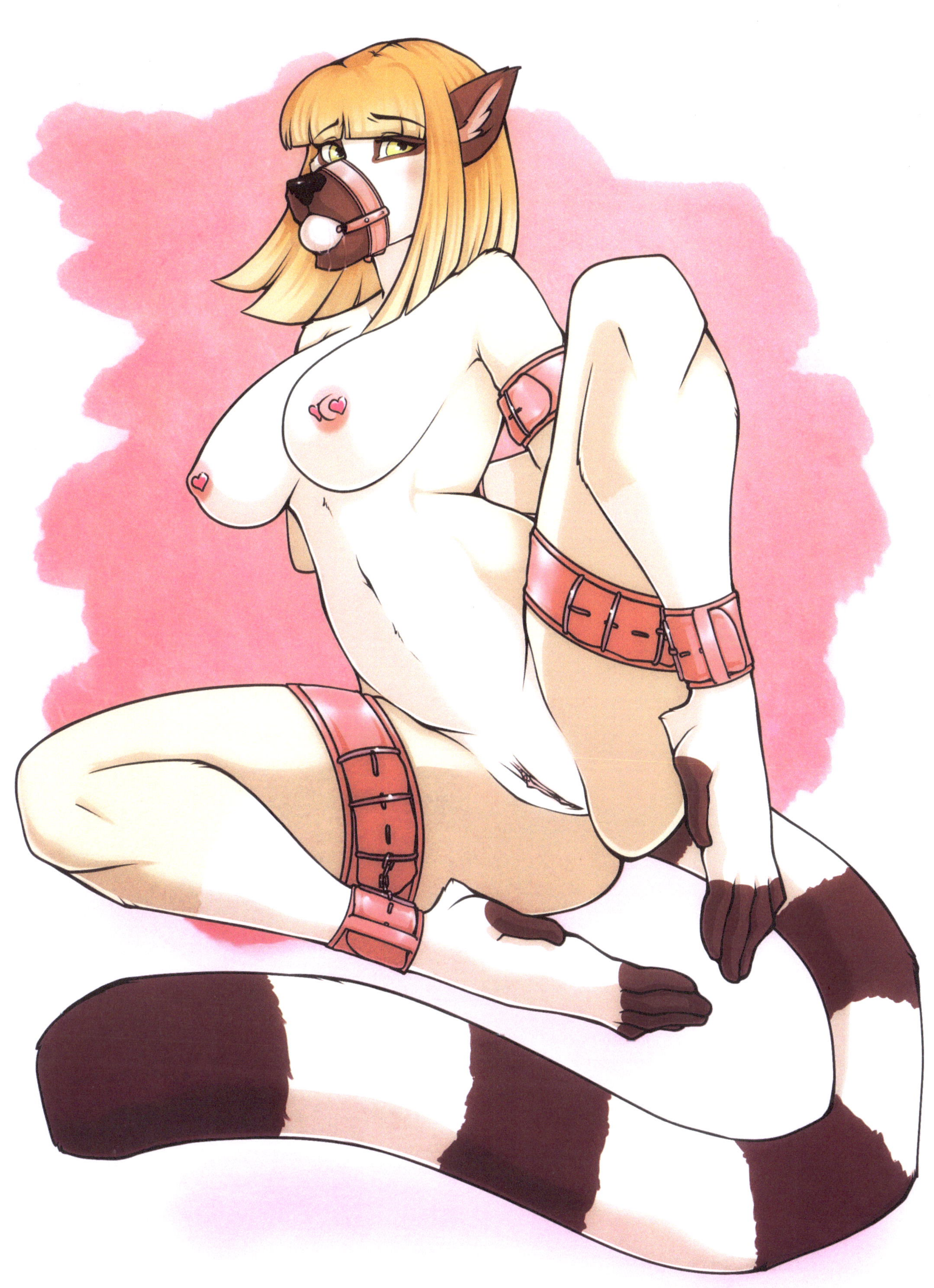

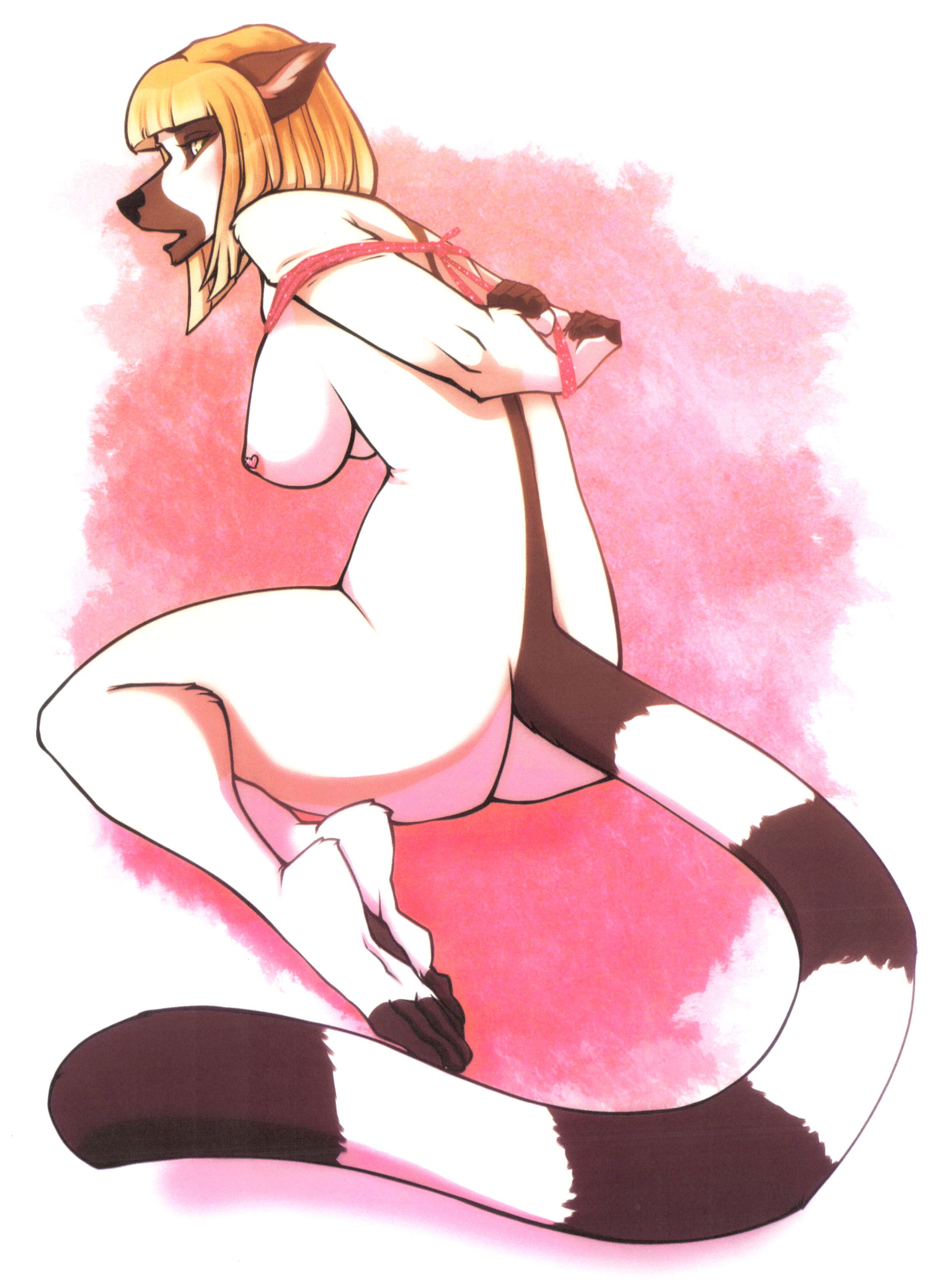

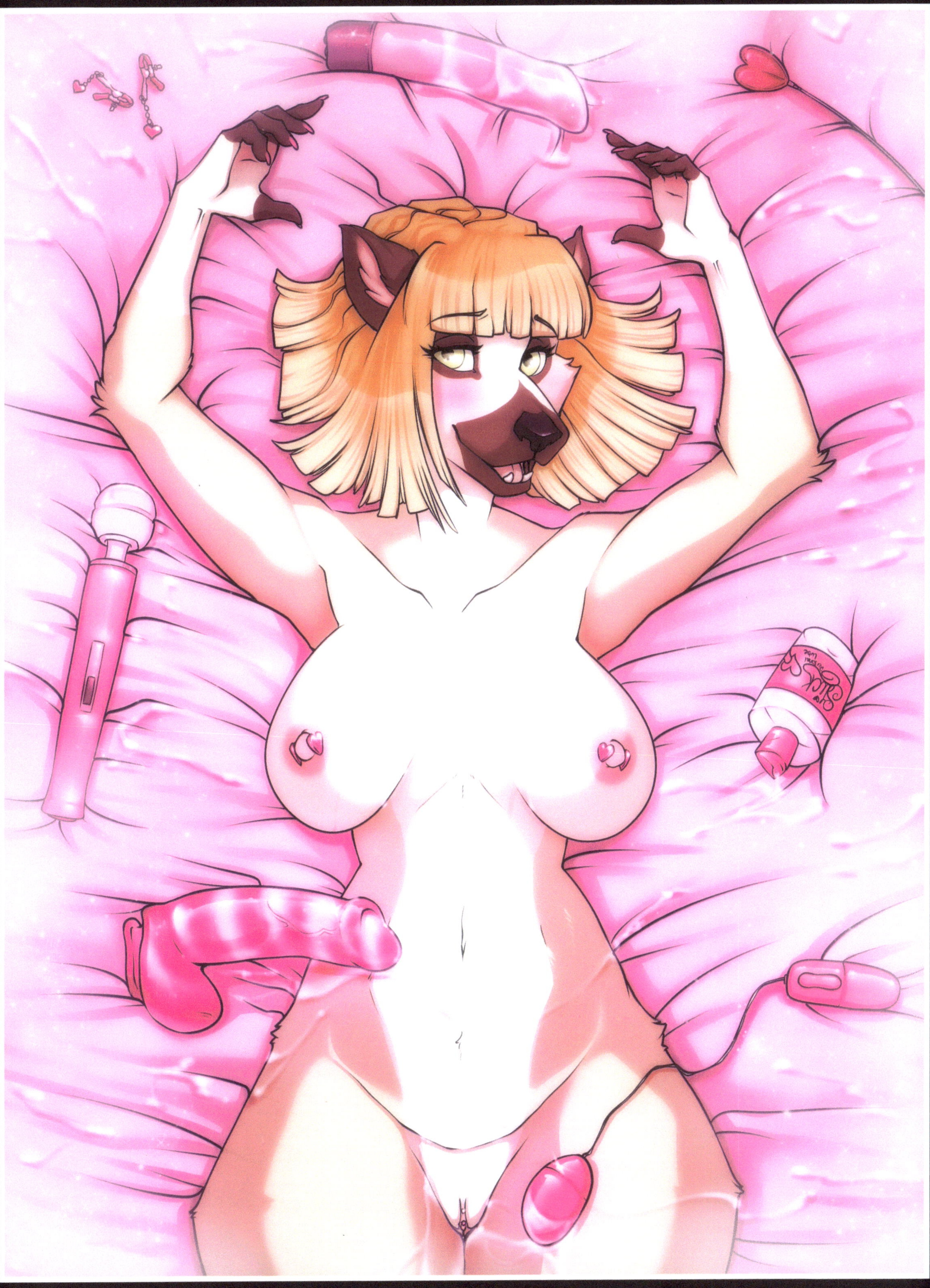

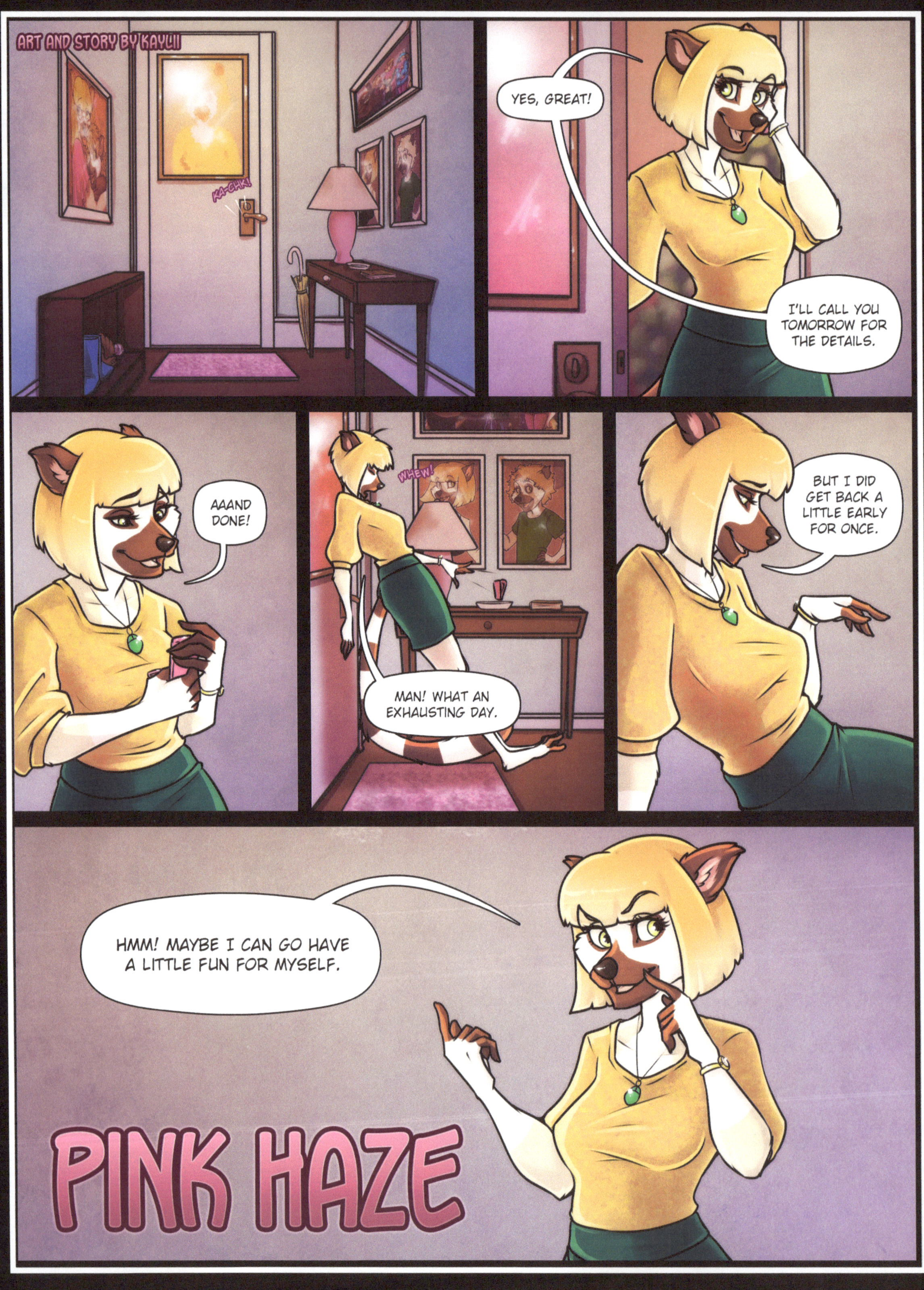
ART AND STORY BY KAYLII
KA-CHK!
YES, GREAT!
I'LL CALL YOU TOMORROW FOR THE DETAILS.
AAAND DONE!
WHEW!
MAN! WHAT AN EXHAUSTING DAY.
BUT I DID GET BACK A LITTLE EARLY FOR ONCE.
HMM! MAYBE I CAN GO HAVE A LITTLE FUN FOR MYSELF.
PINK HAZE

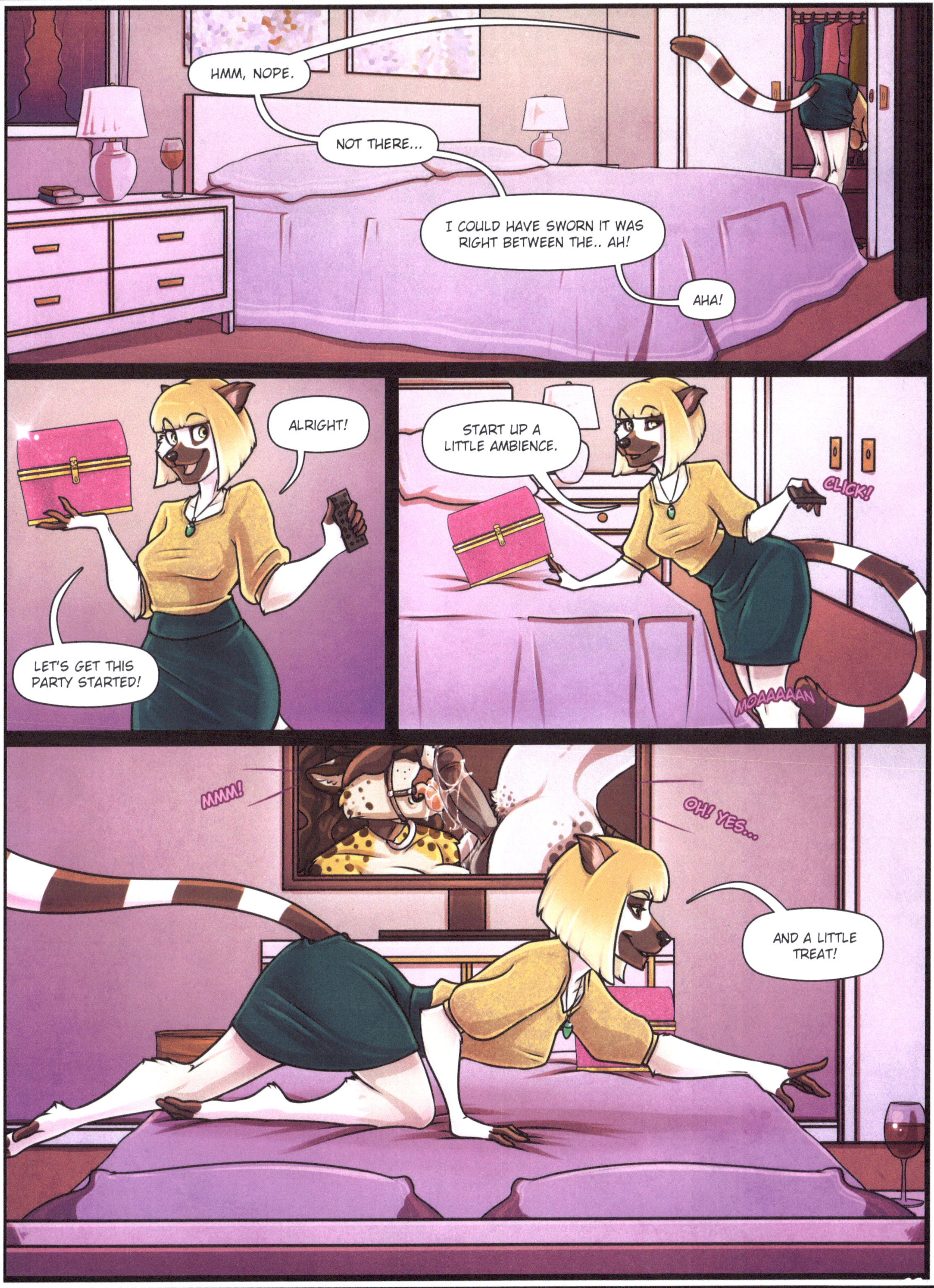
HMM, NOPE.
NOT THERE...
I COULD HAVE SWORN IT WAS RIGHT BETWEEN THE.. AH!
AHA!
ALRIGHT!
LET'S GET THIS PARTY STARTED!
START UP A LITTLE AMBIENCE.
CLICK!
MOAAAAAN
MMM!
OH! YES...
AND A LITTLE TREAT!

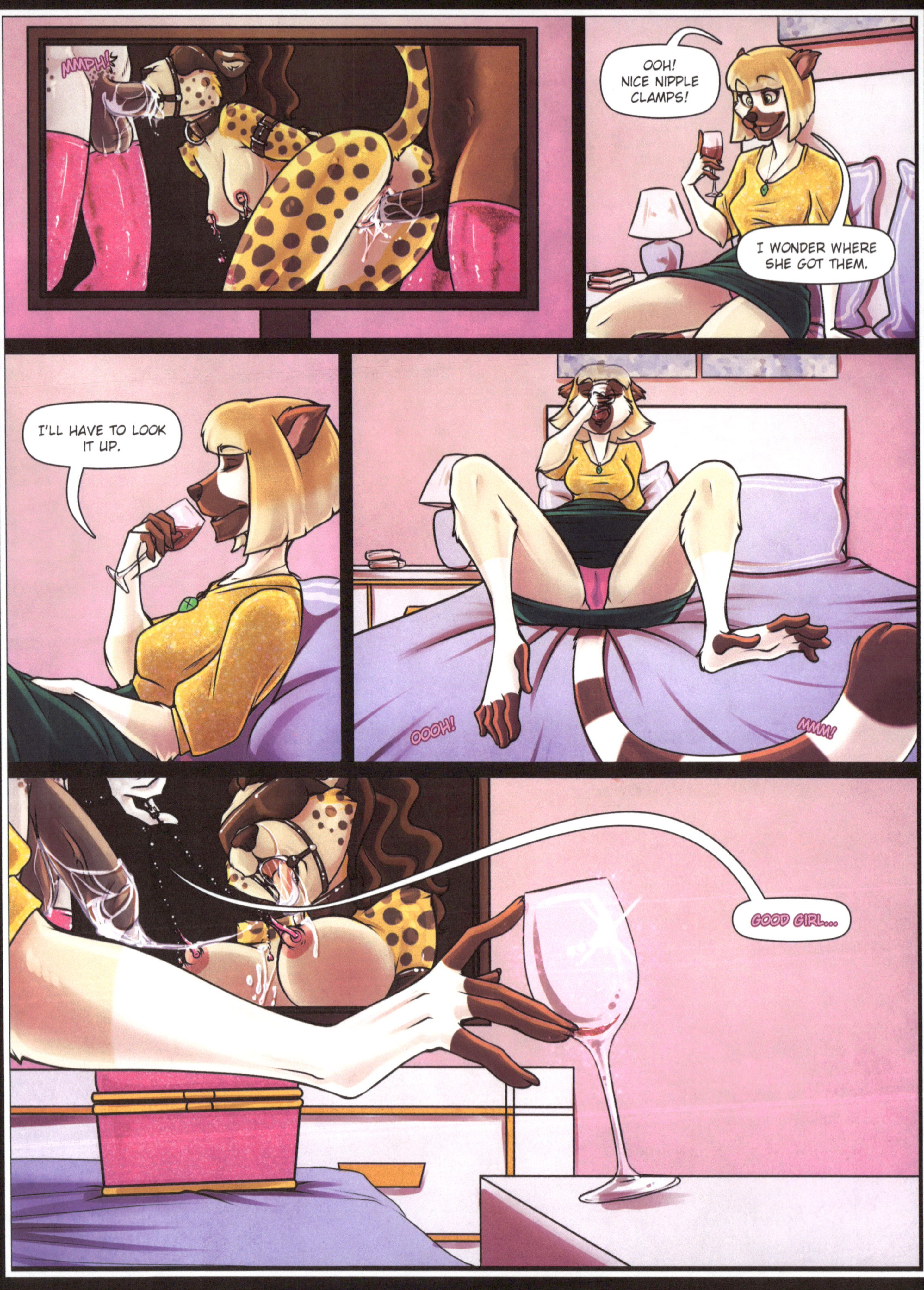
MMPH!
OOH! NICE NIPPLE CLAMPS!
I WONDER WHERE SHE GOT THEM.
I'LL HAVE TO LOOK IT UP.
OOOH!
MMM!
GOOD GIRL...

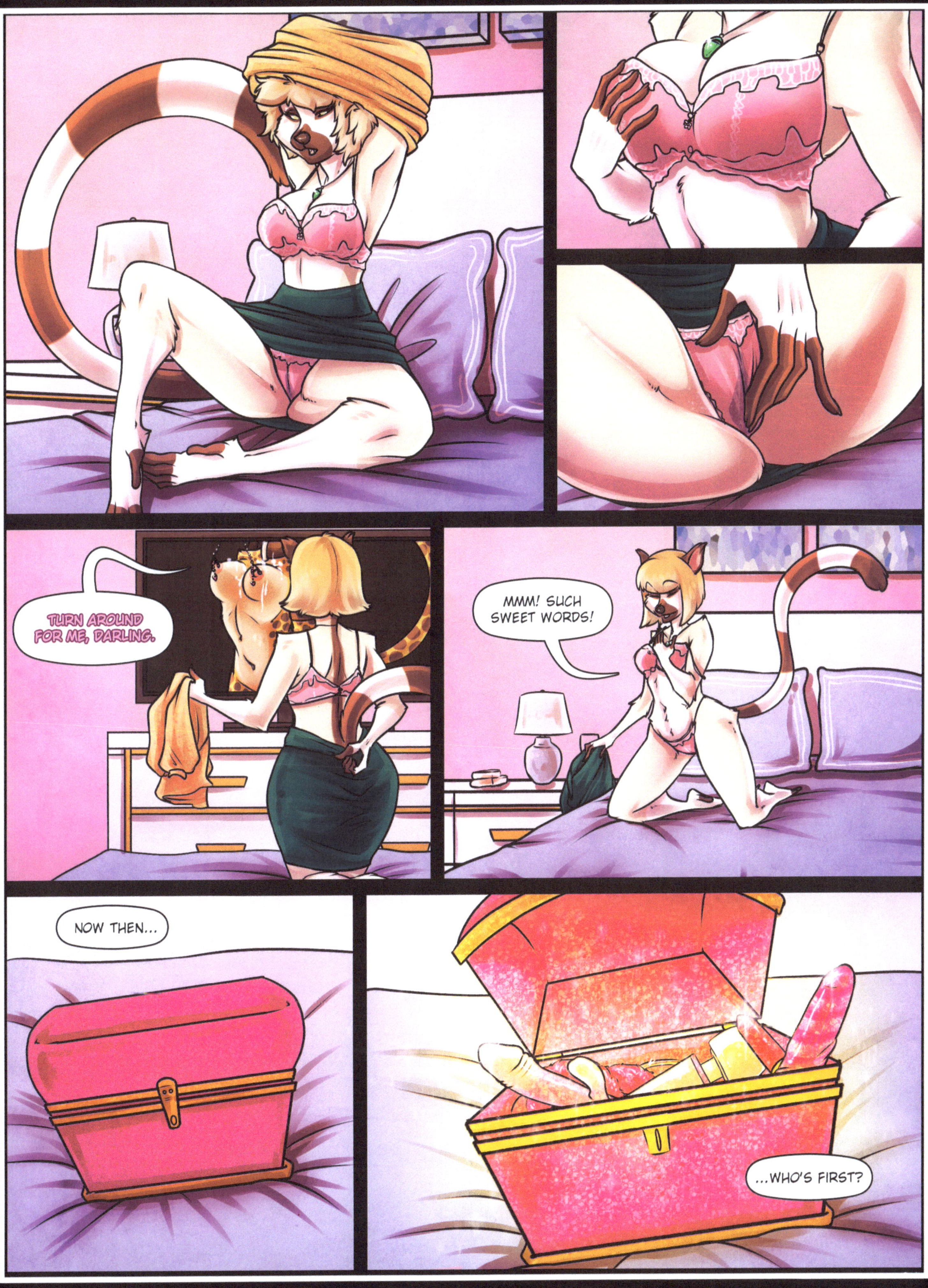
TURN AROUND FOR ME, DARLING.
MMM! SUCH SWEET WORDS!
NOW THEN...
...WHO'S FIRST?

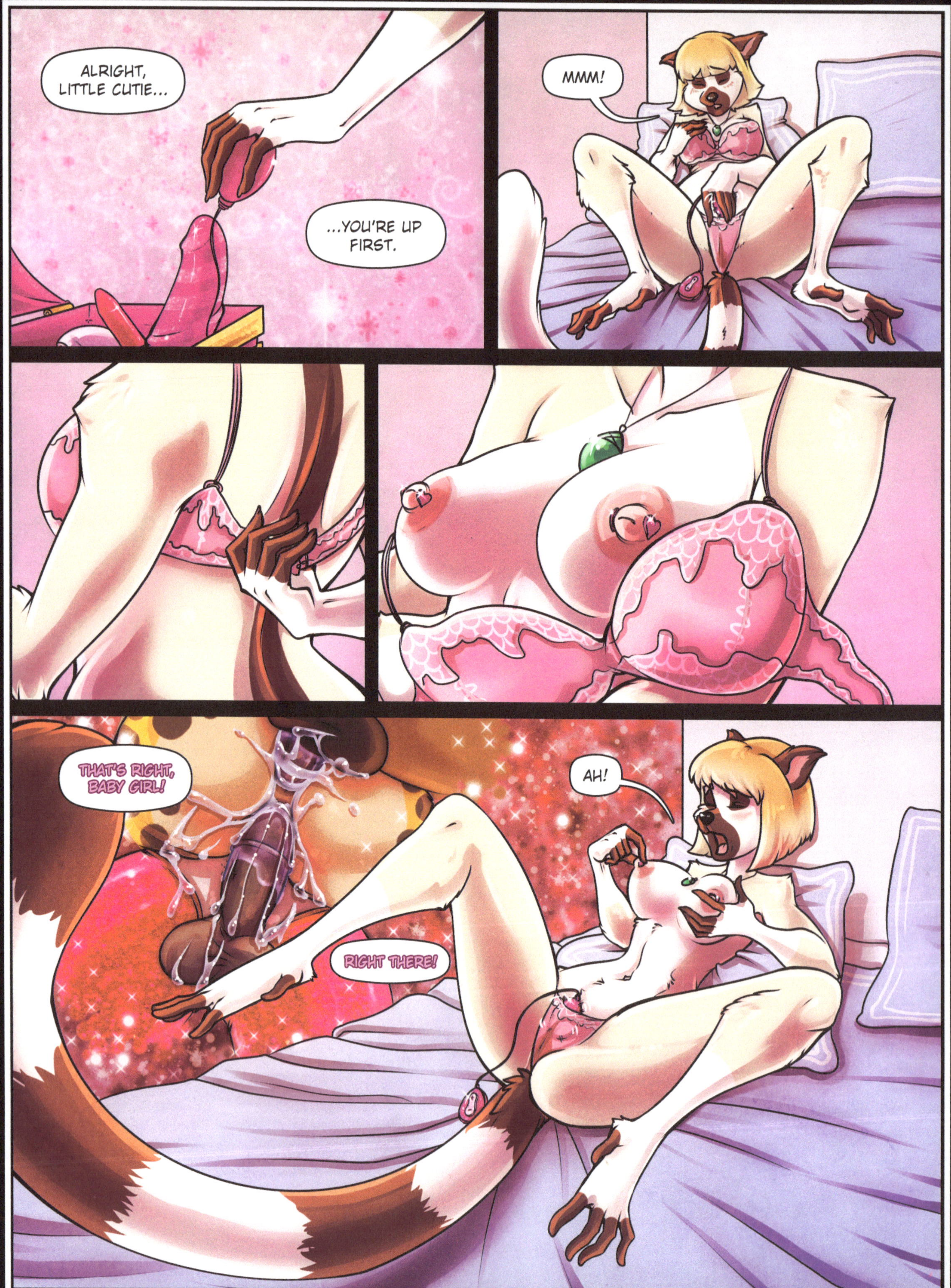

ALRIGHT, LITTLE CUTIE...
...YOU'RE UP FIRST.
MMM!
THAT'S RIGHT, BABY GIRL!
AH!
RIGHT THERE!

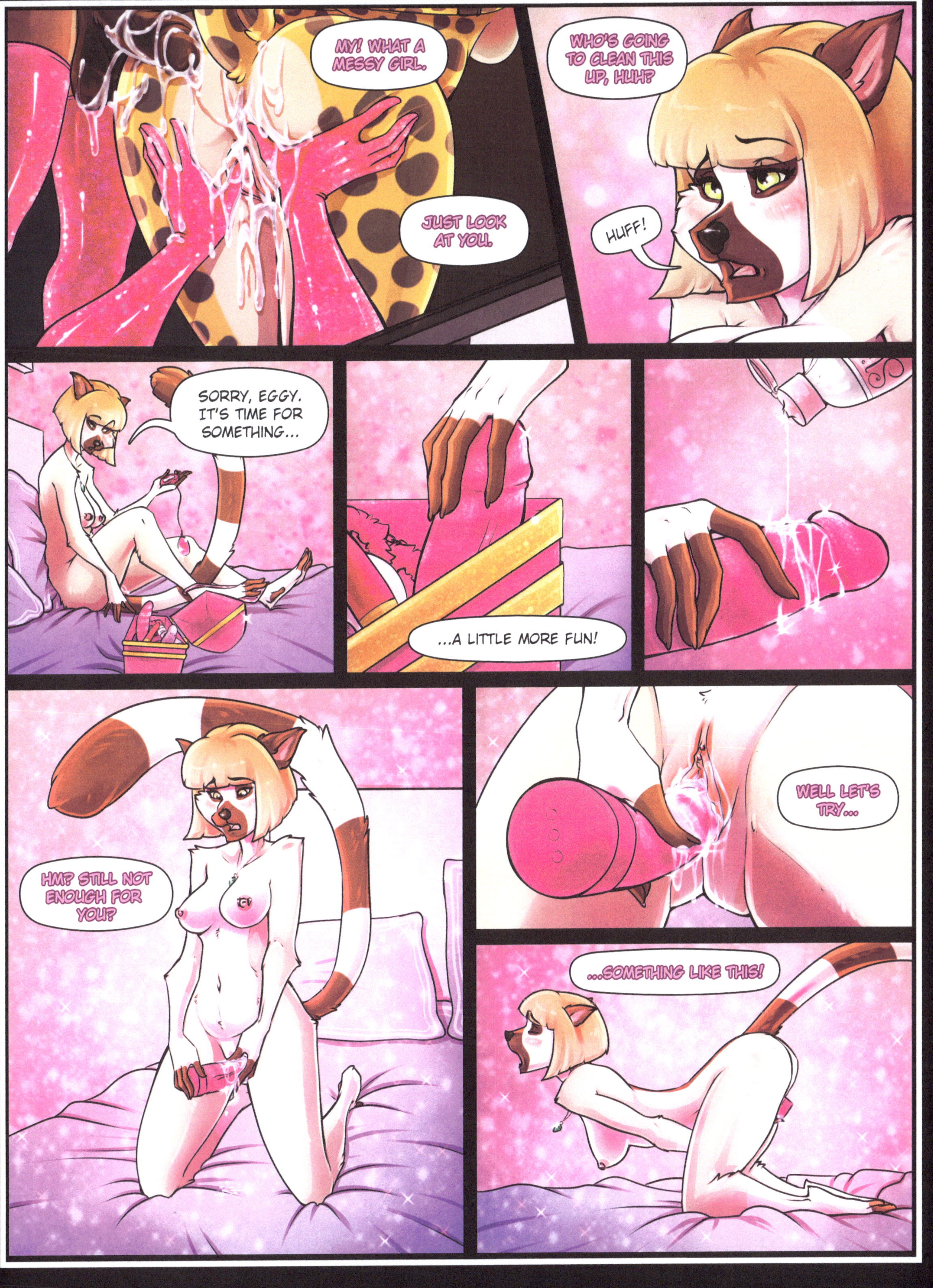
MY! WHAT A MESSY GIRL.
JUST LOOK AT YOU.
WHO'S GOING TO CLEAN THIS UP, HUH?
HUFF!
SORRY, EGGY. IT'S TIME FOR SOMETHING...
...A LITTLE MORE FUN!
HM? STILL NOT ENOUGH FOR YOU?
WELL LET'S TRY...
...SOMETHING LIKE THIS!

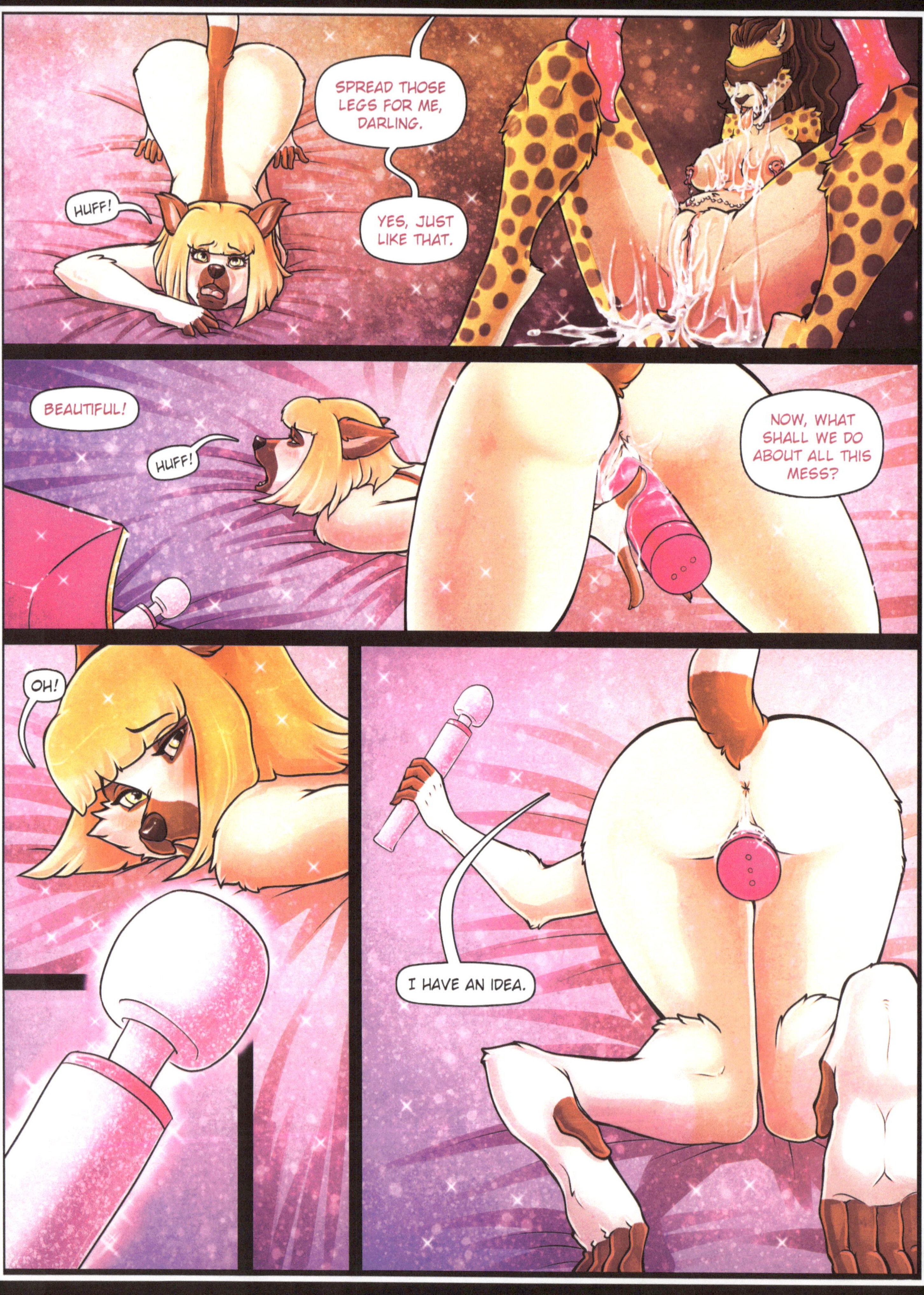
SPREAD THOSE LEGS FOR ME, DARLING.
HUFF!
YES, JUST LIKE THAT.
BEAUTIFUL!
HUFF!
NOW, WHAT SHALL WE DO ABOUT ALL THIS MESS?
OH!
I HAVE AN IDEA.

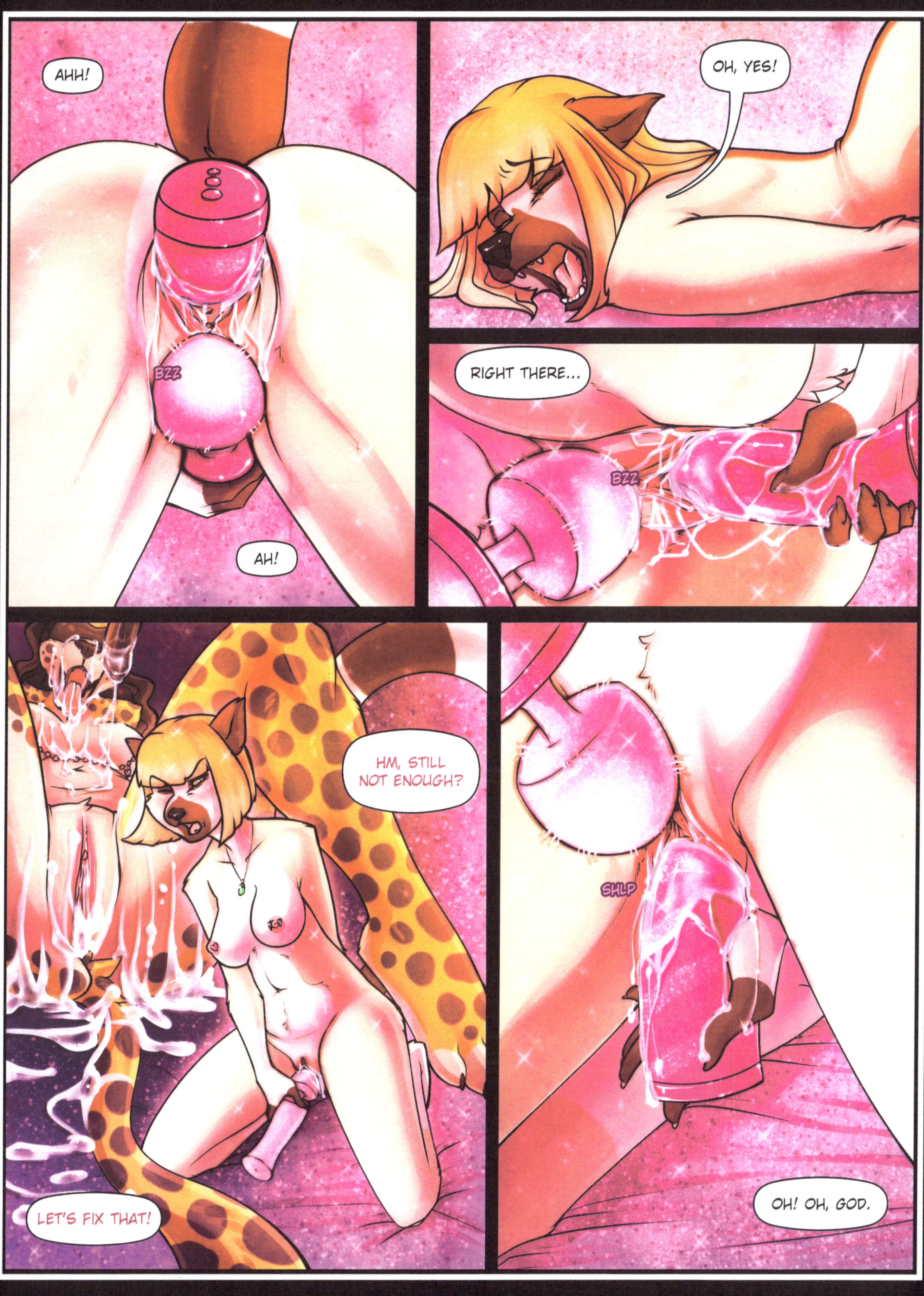
AHH!
BZZ
AH!
OH, YES!
RIGHT THERE...
BZZ
HM, STILL NOT ENOUGH?
LET'S FIX THAT!
SHLP
OH! OH, GOD.

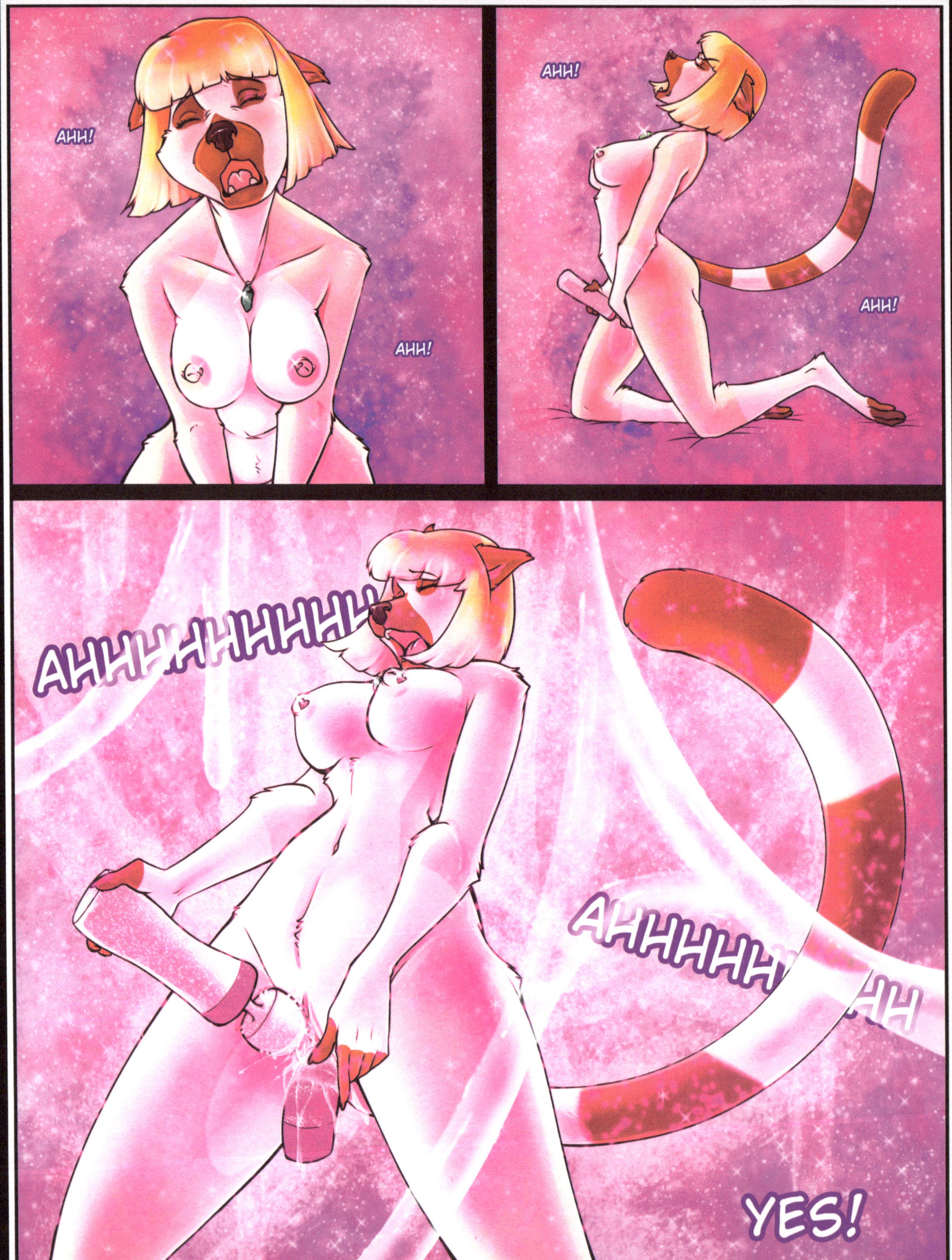
AHH!
AHH!
AHH!
AHH!
AHHHHHHHHHH
AHHHHHHHHHH
YES!

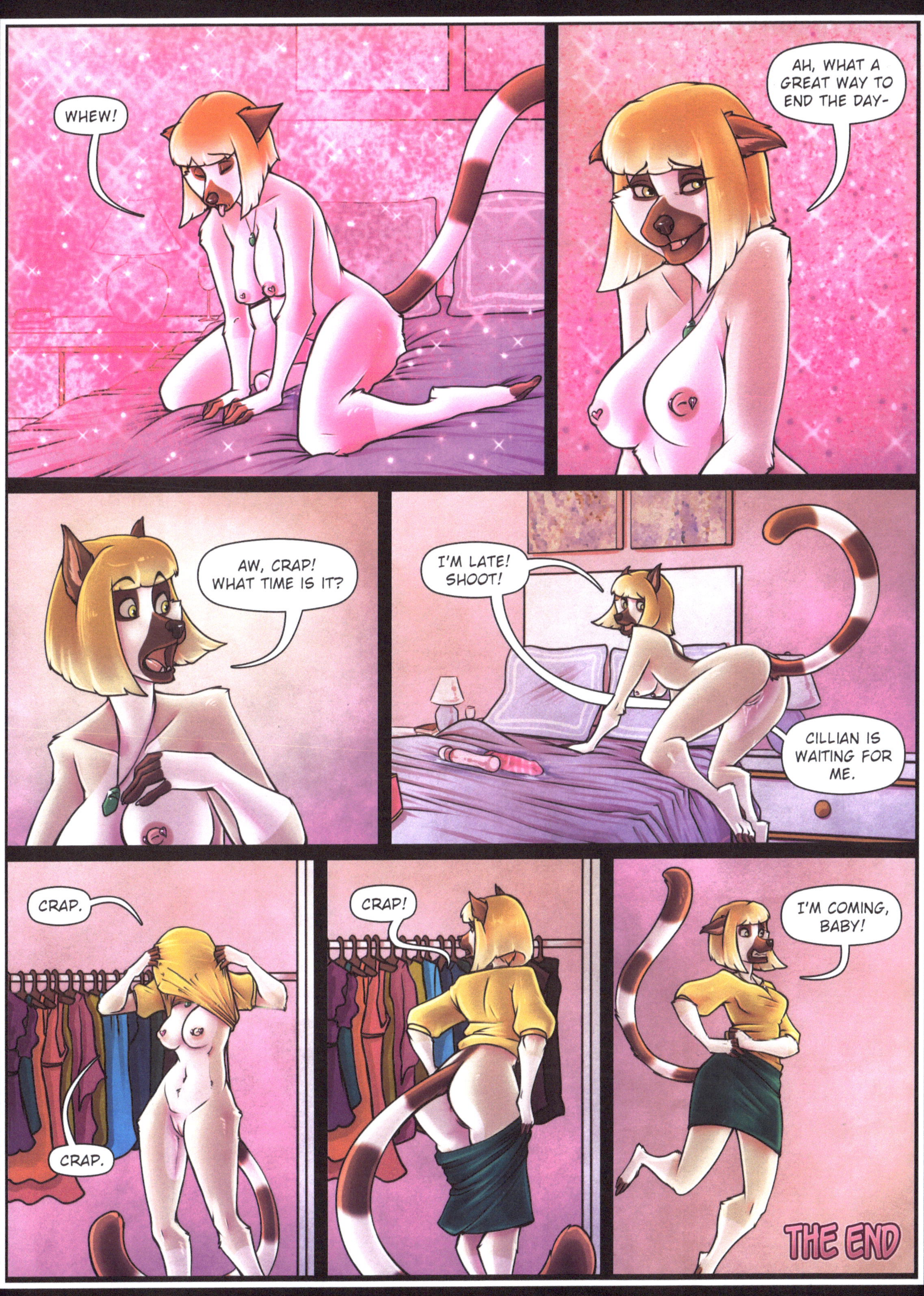
WHEW!
AH, WHAT A GREAT WAY TO END THE DAY-
AW, CRAP! WHAT TIME IS IT?
I'M LATE! SHOOT!
CILLIAN IS WAITING FOR ME.
CRAP.
CRAP.
CRAP!
I'M COMING, BABY!
THE END

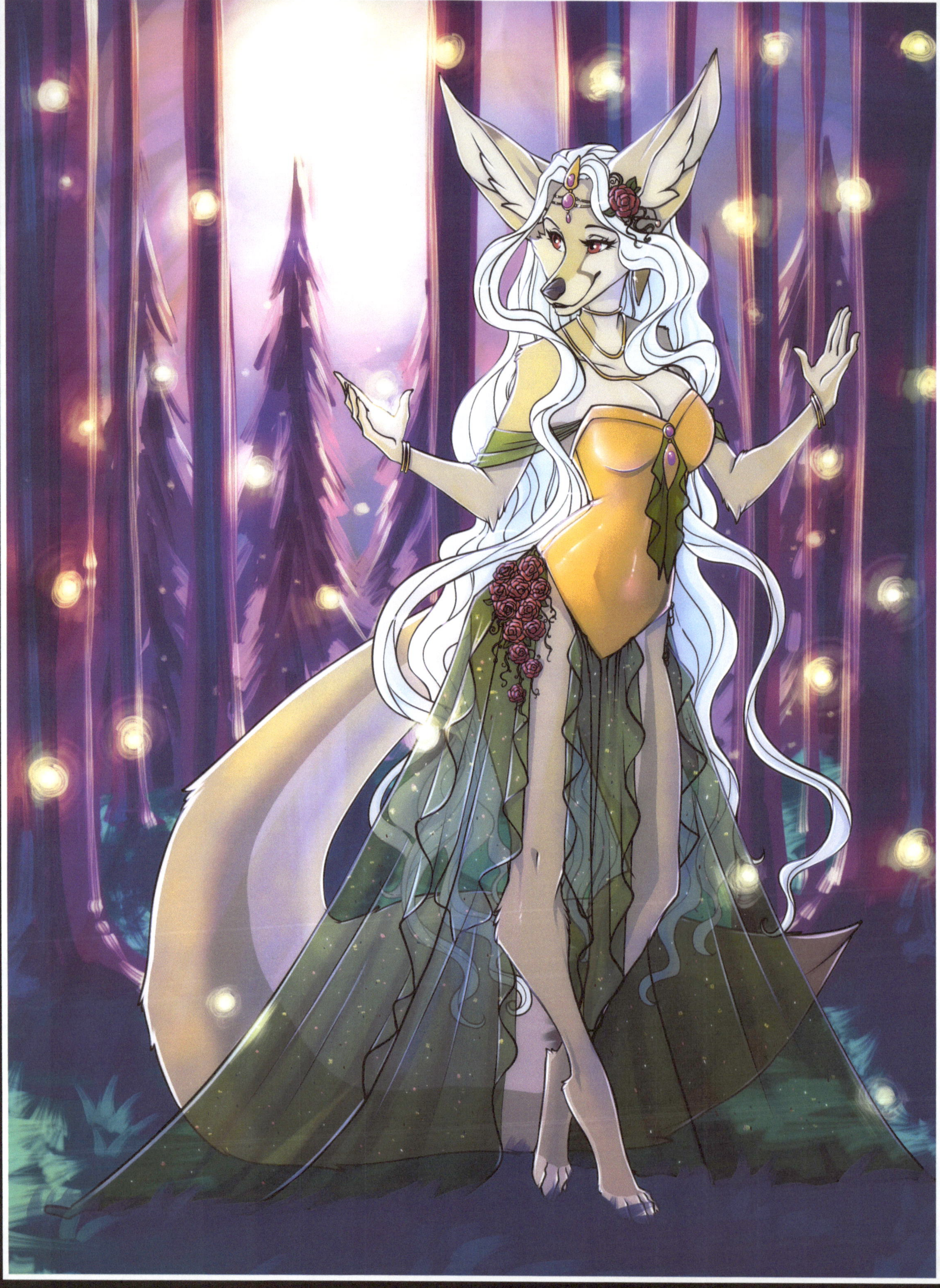

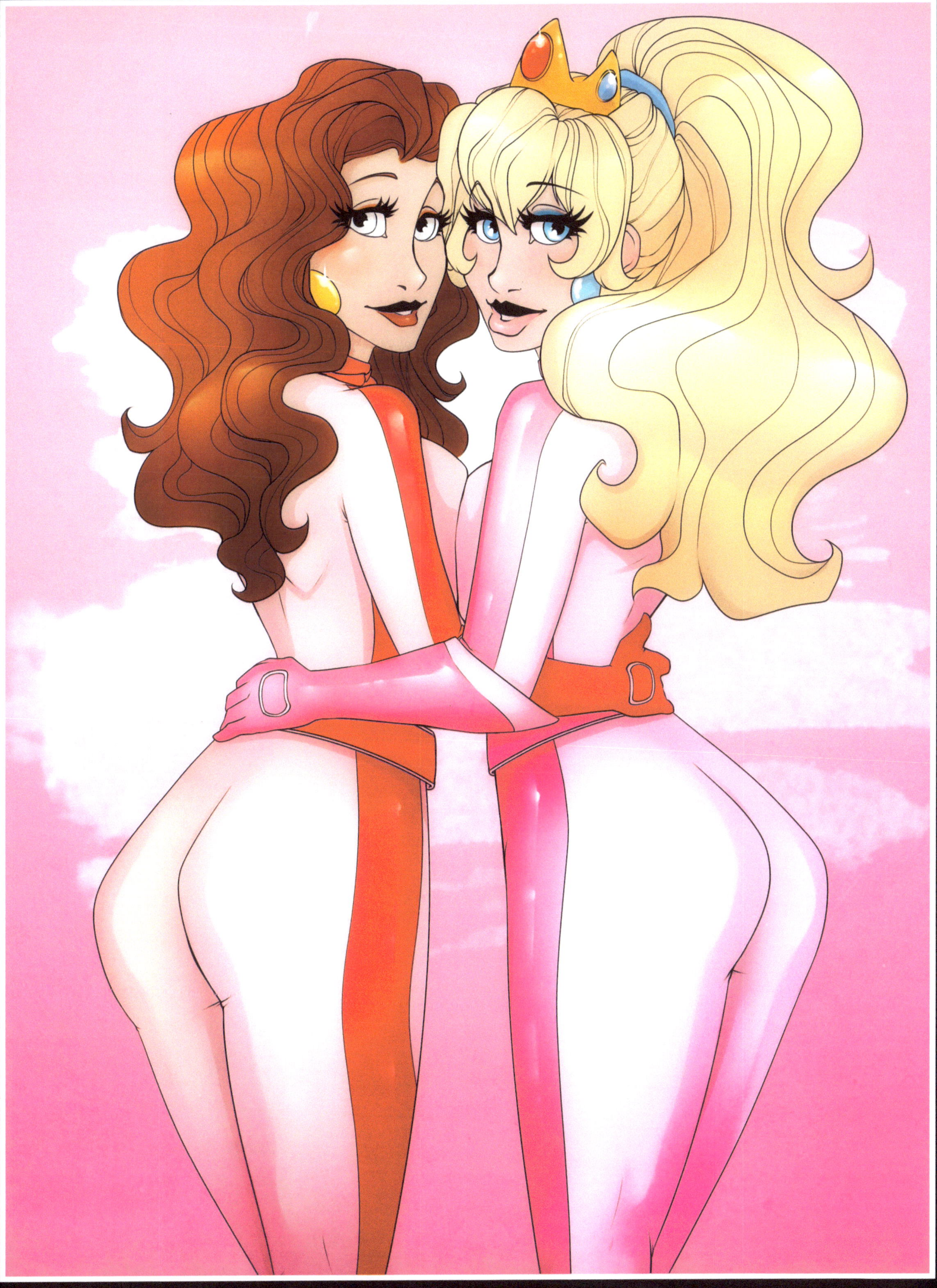

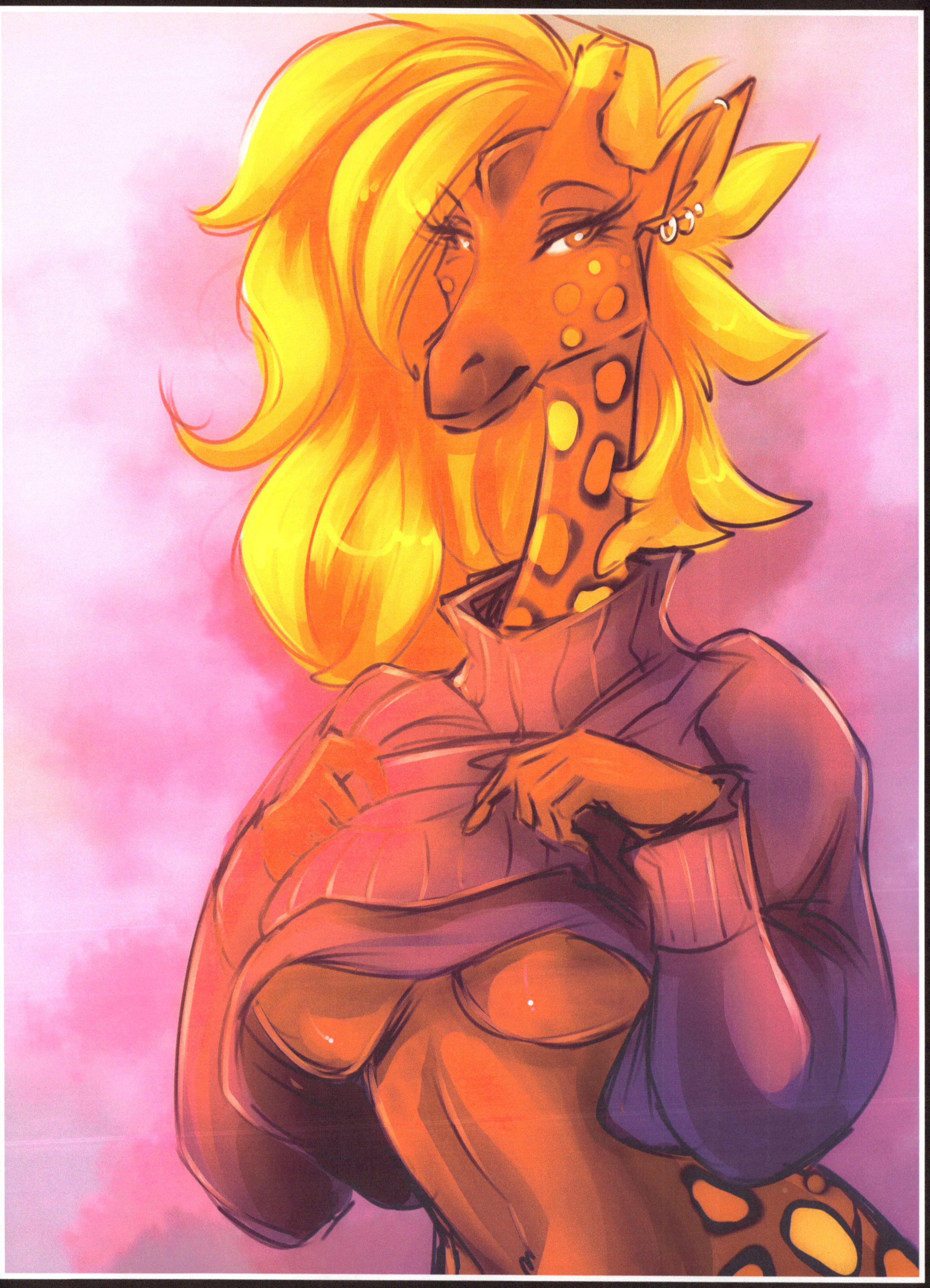

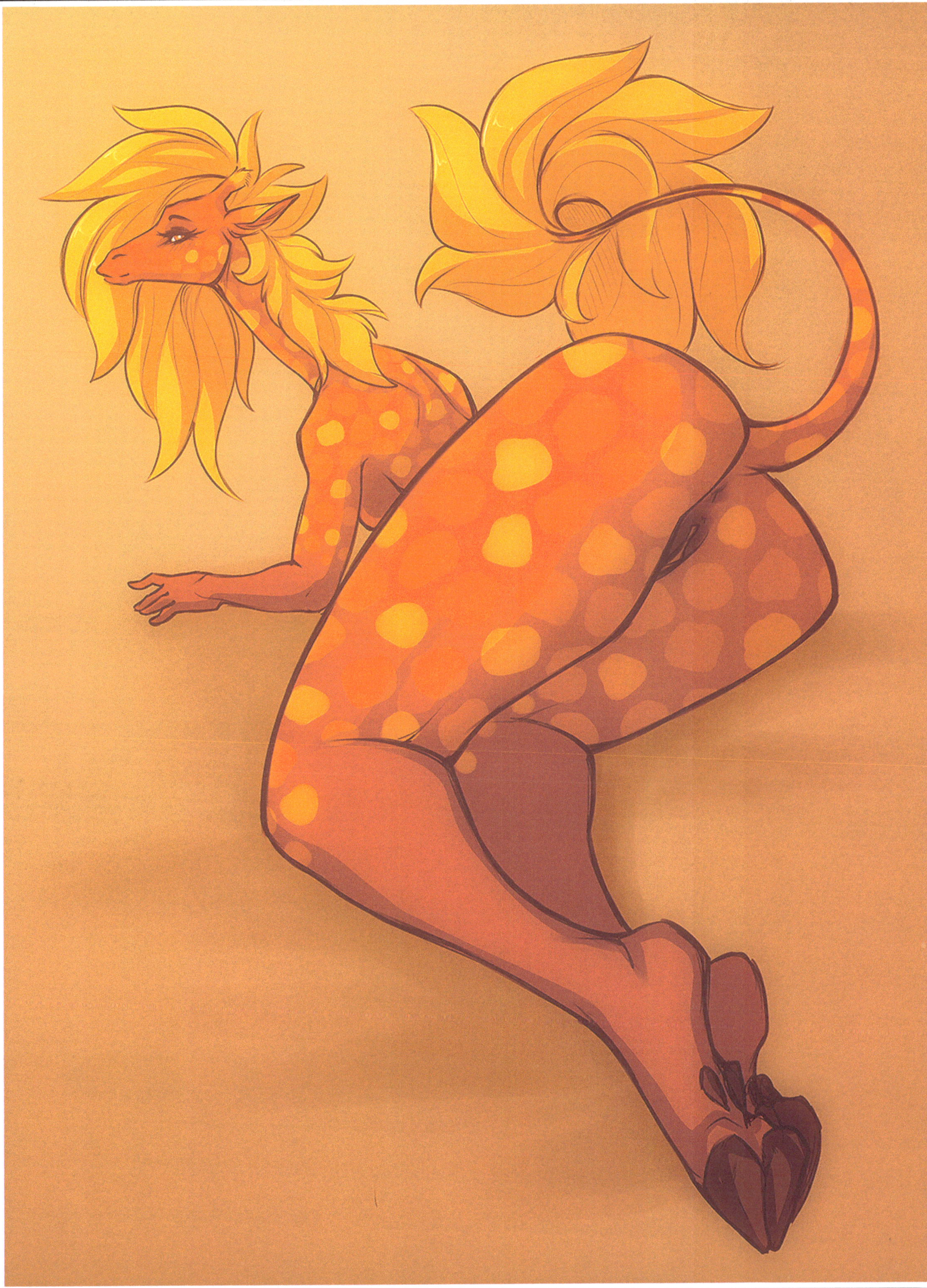

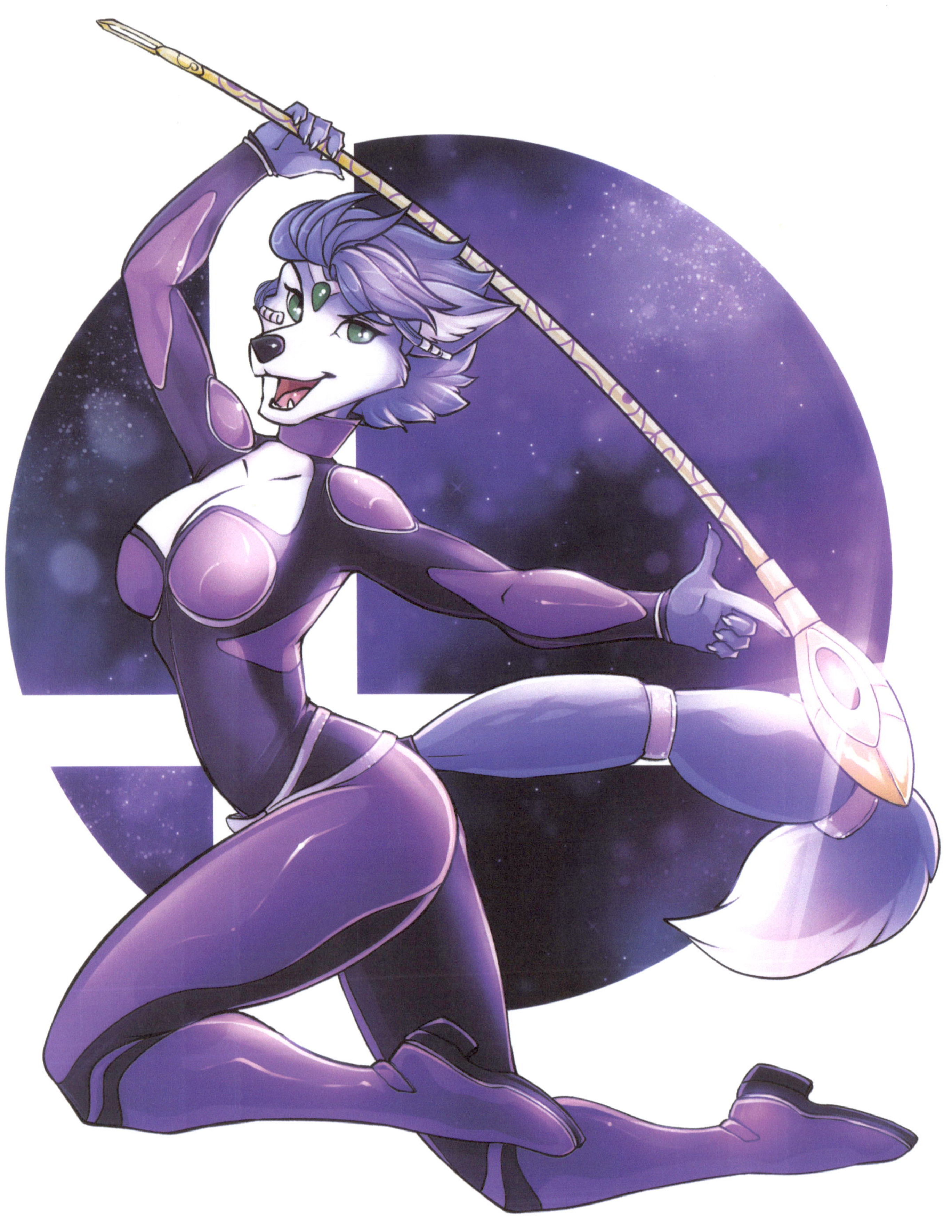

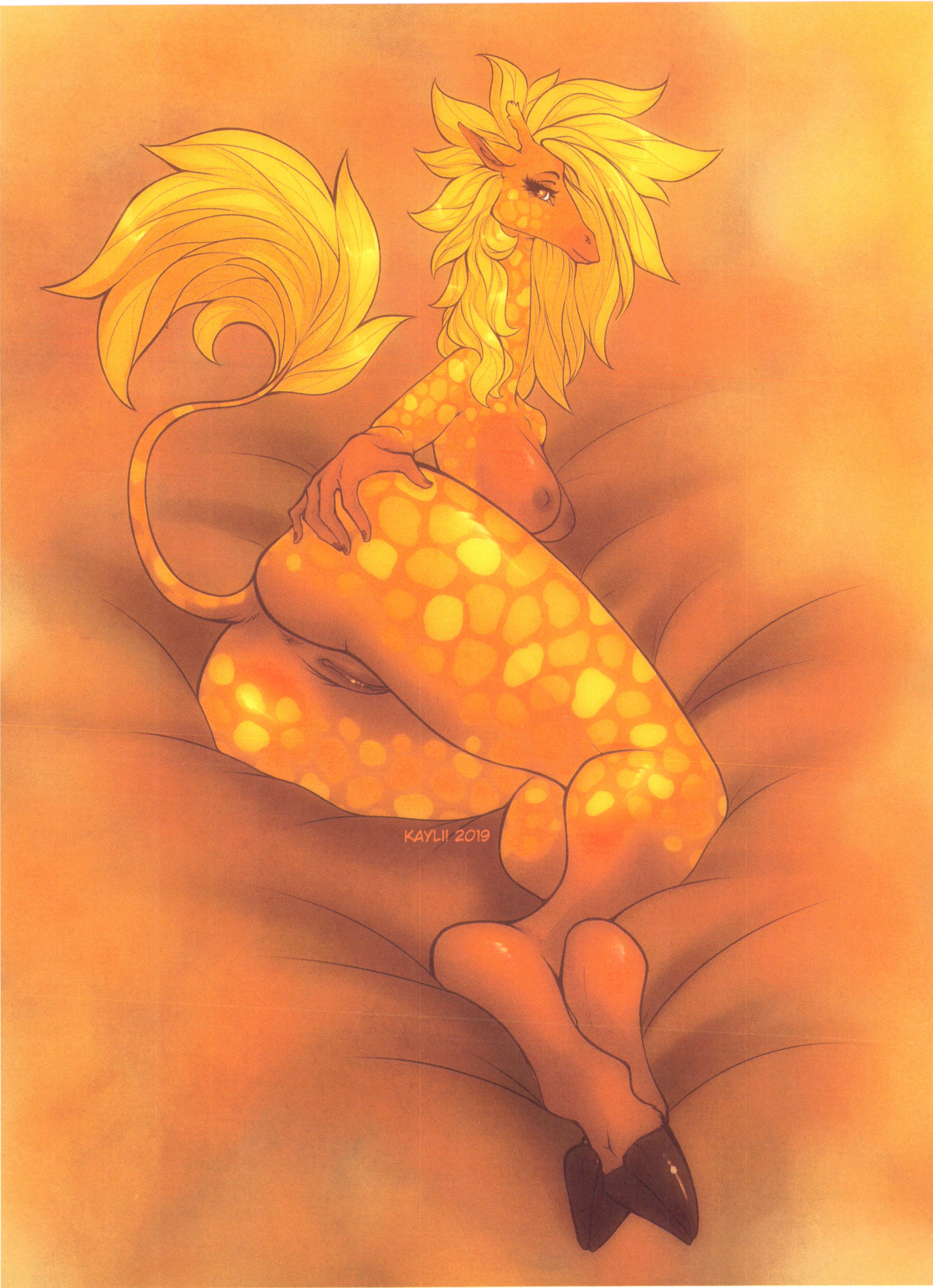
KAYLII 2019

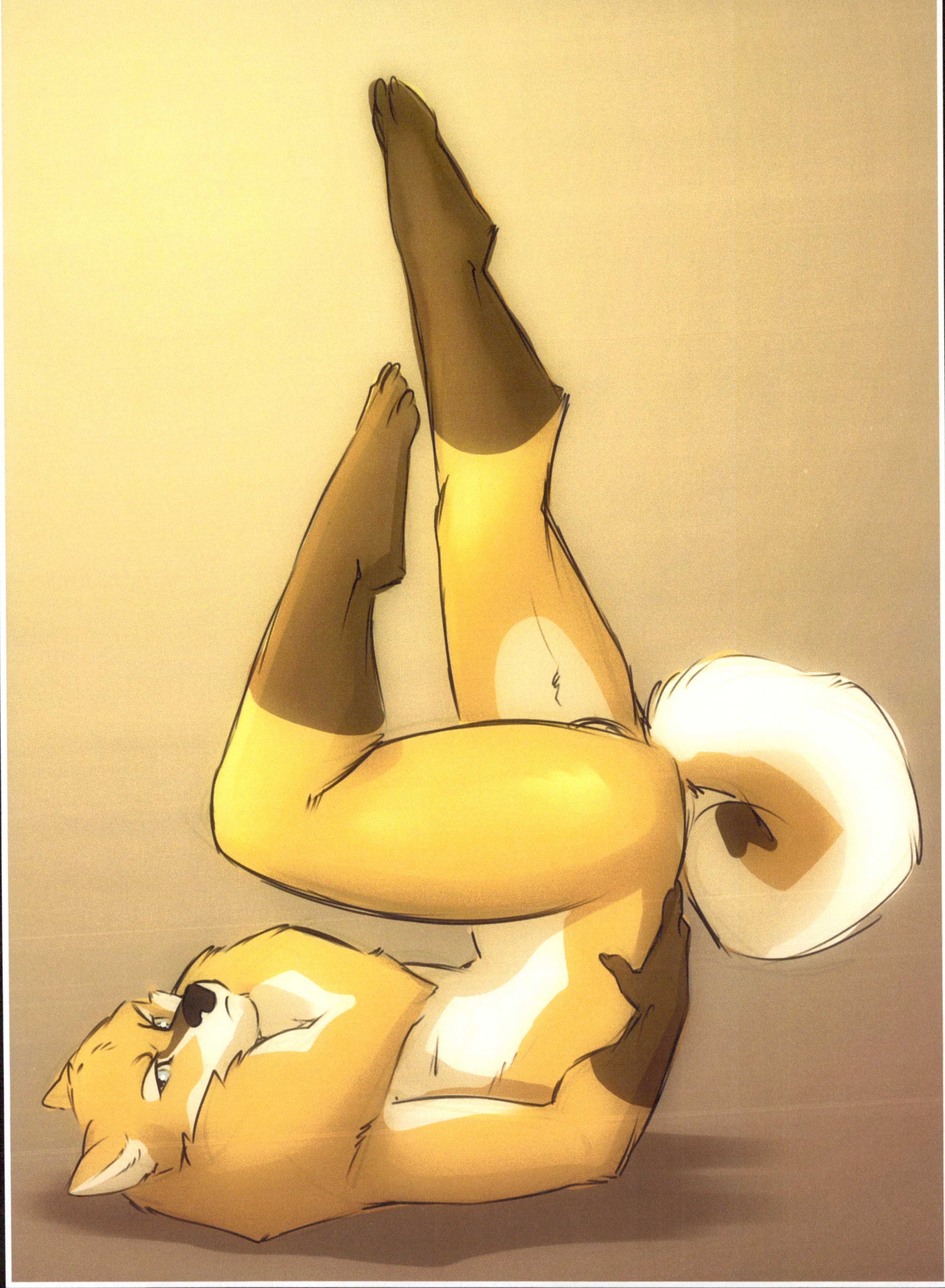

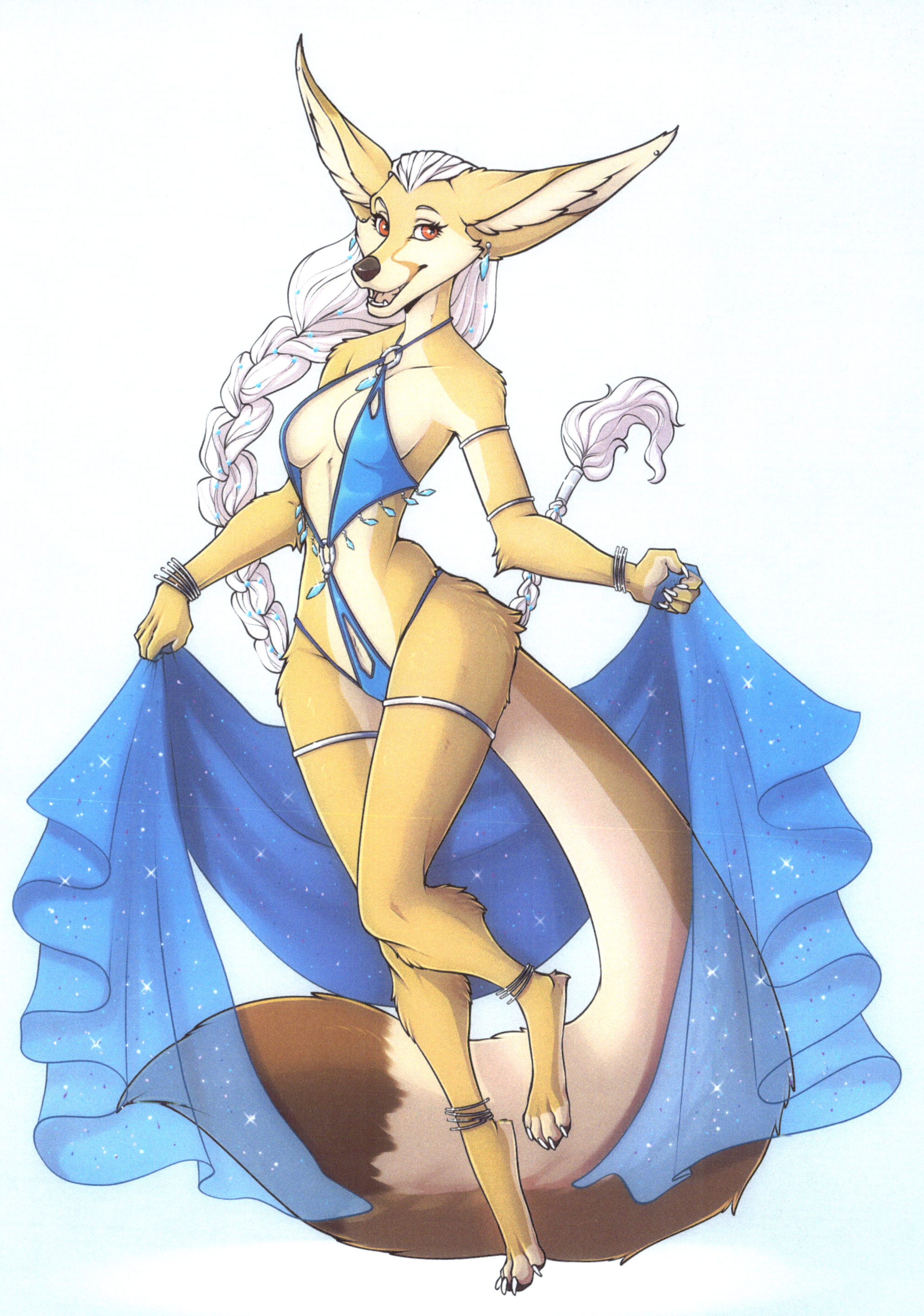

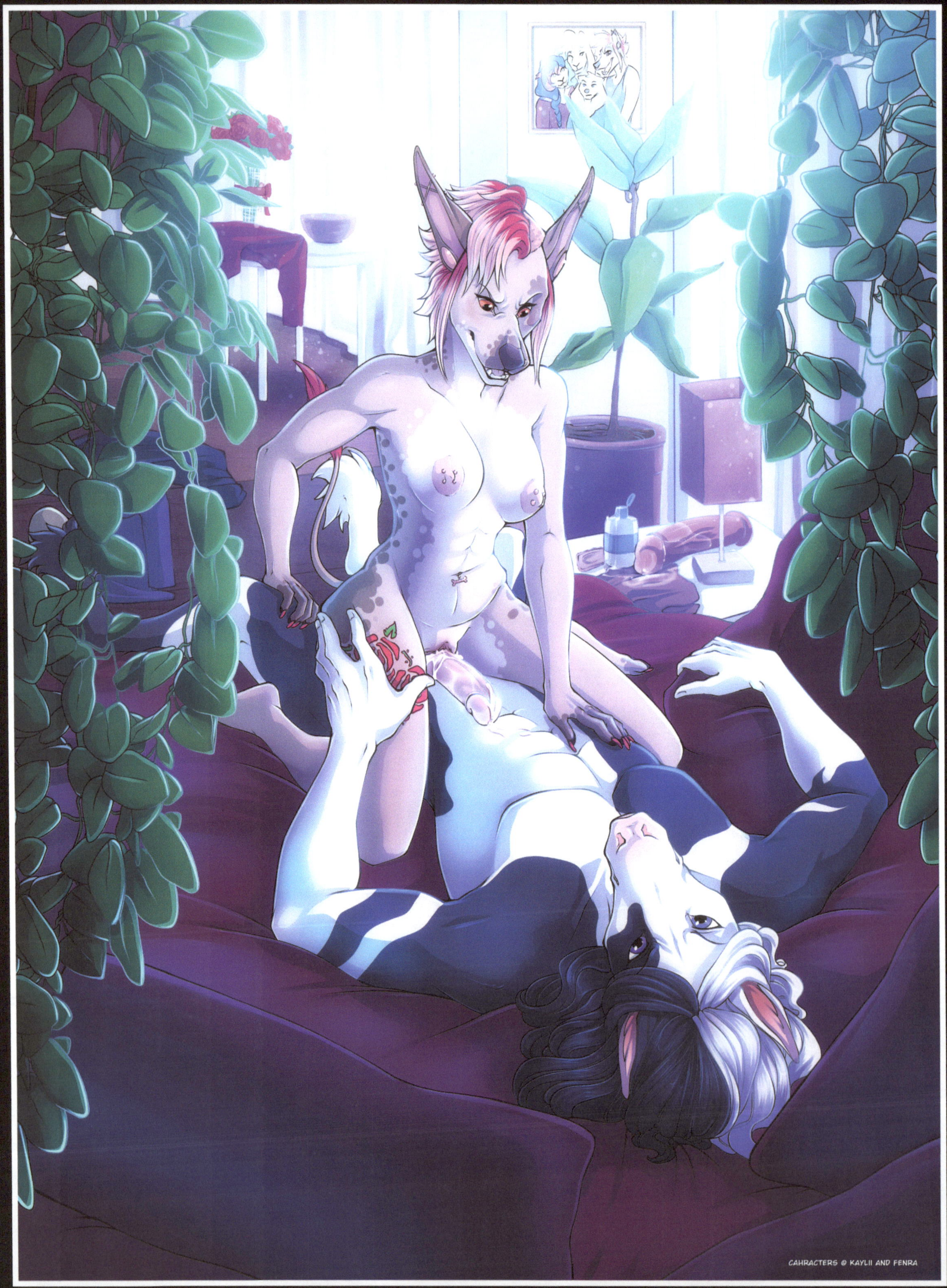
CAHRACTERS © KAYLII AND FENRA

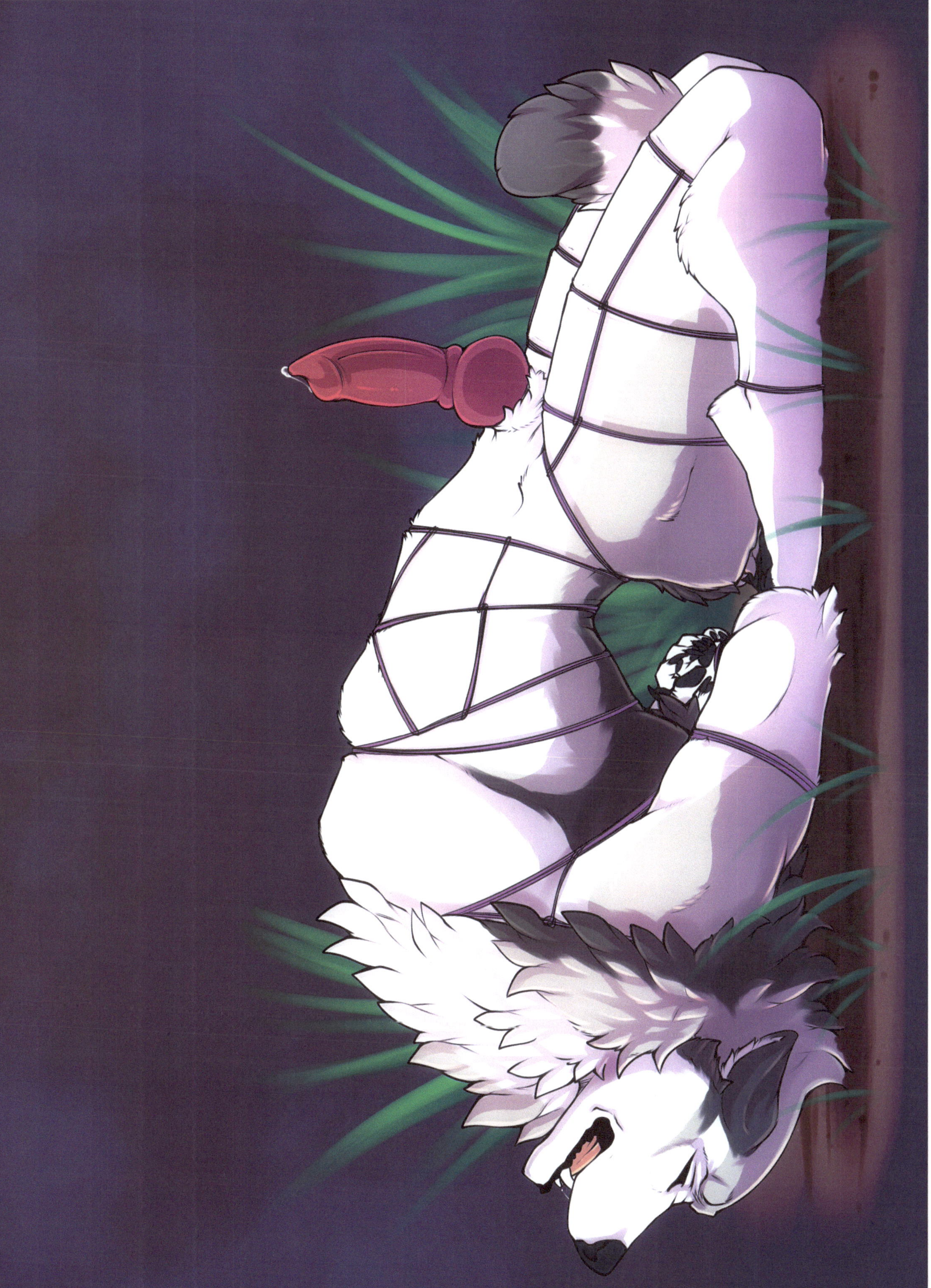

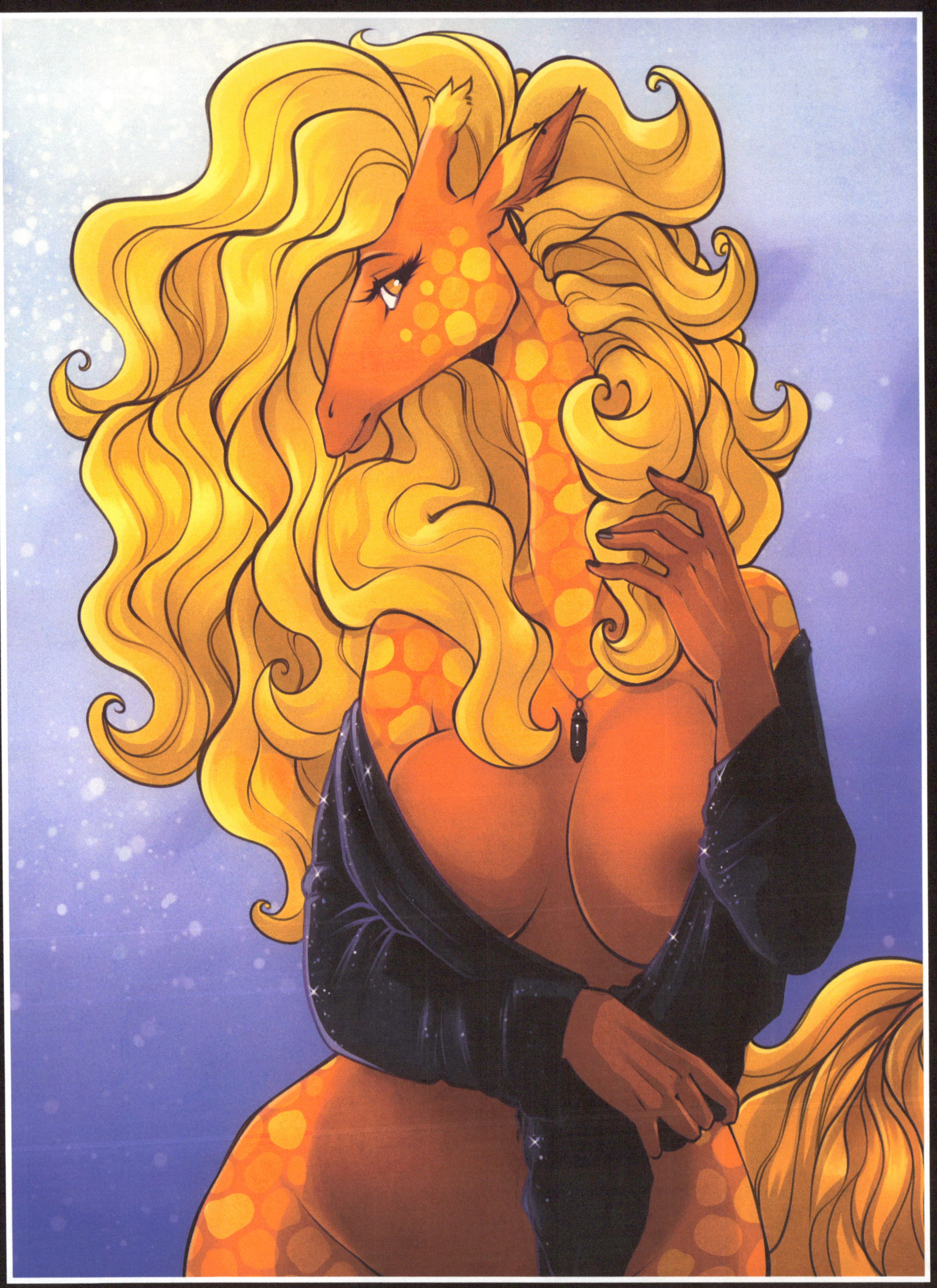

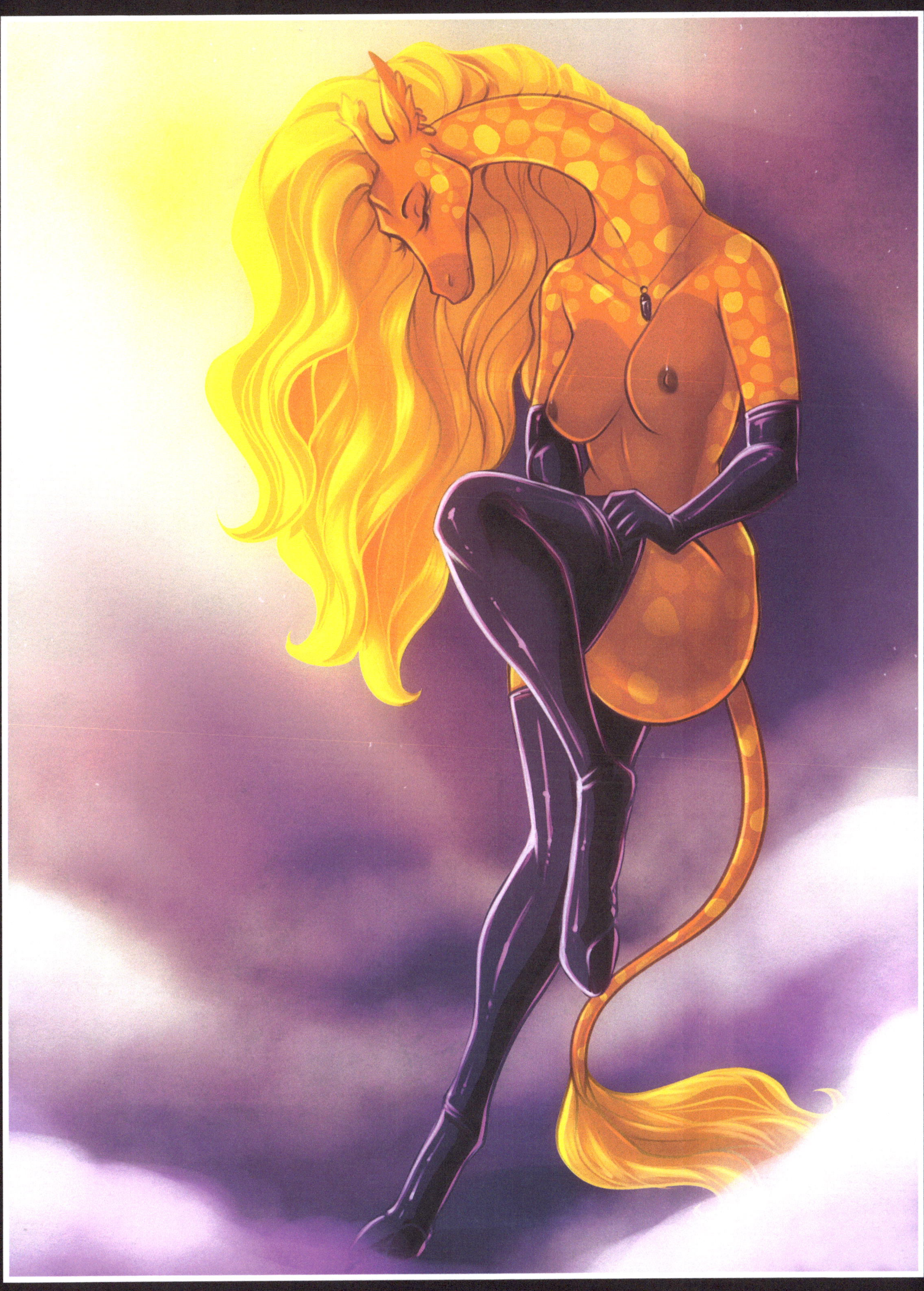

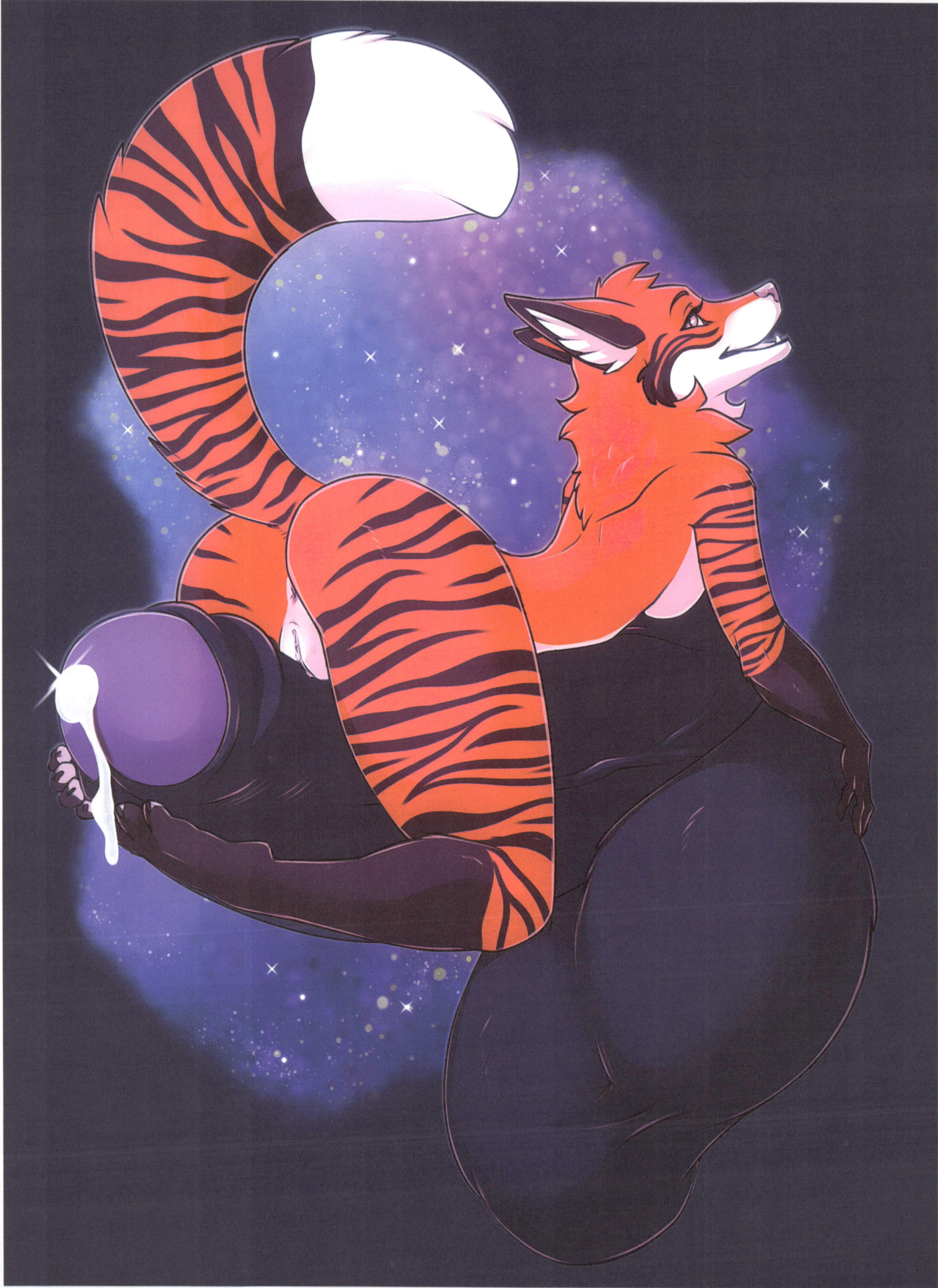

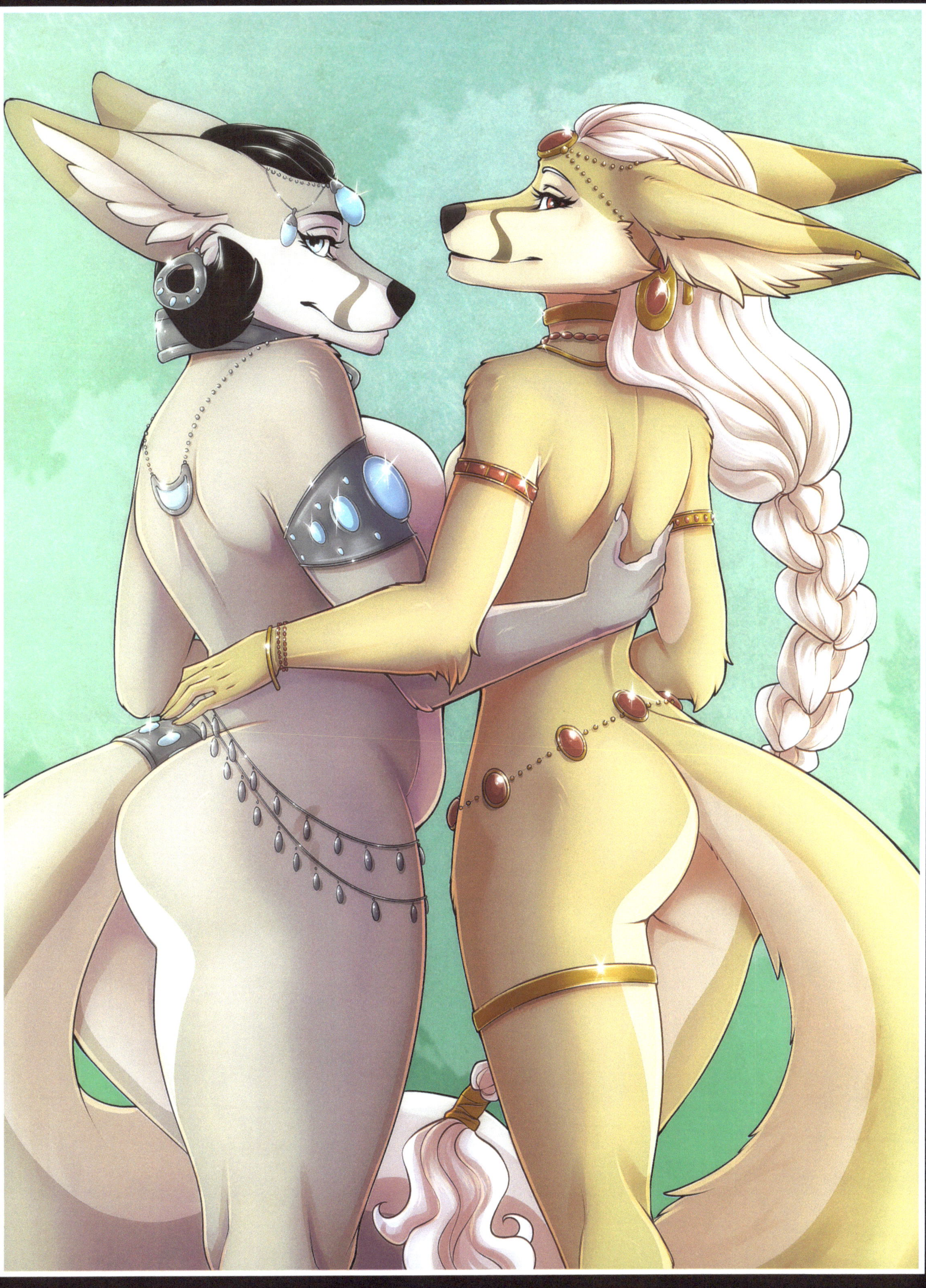

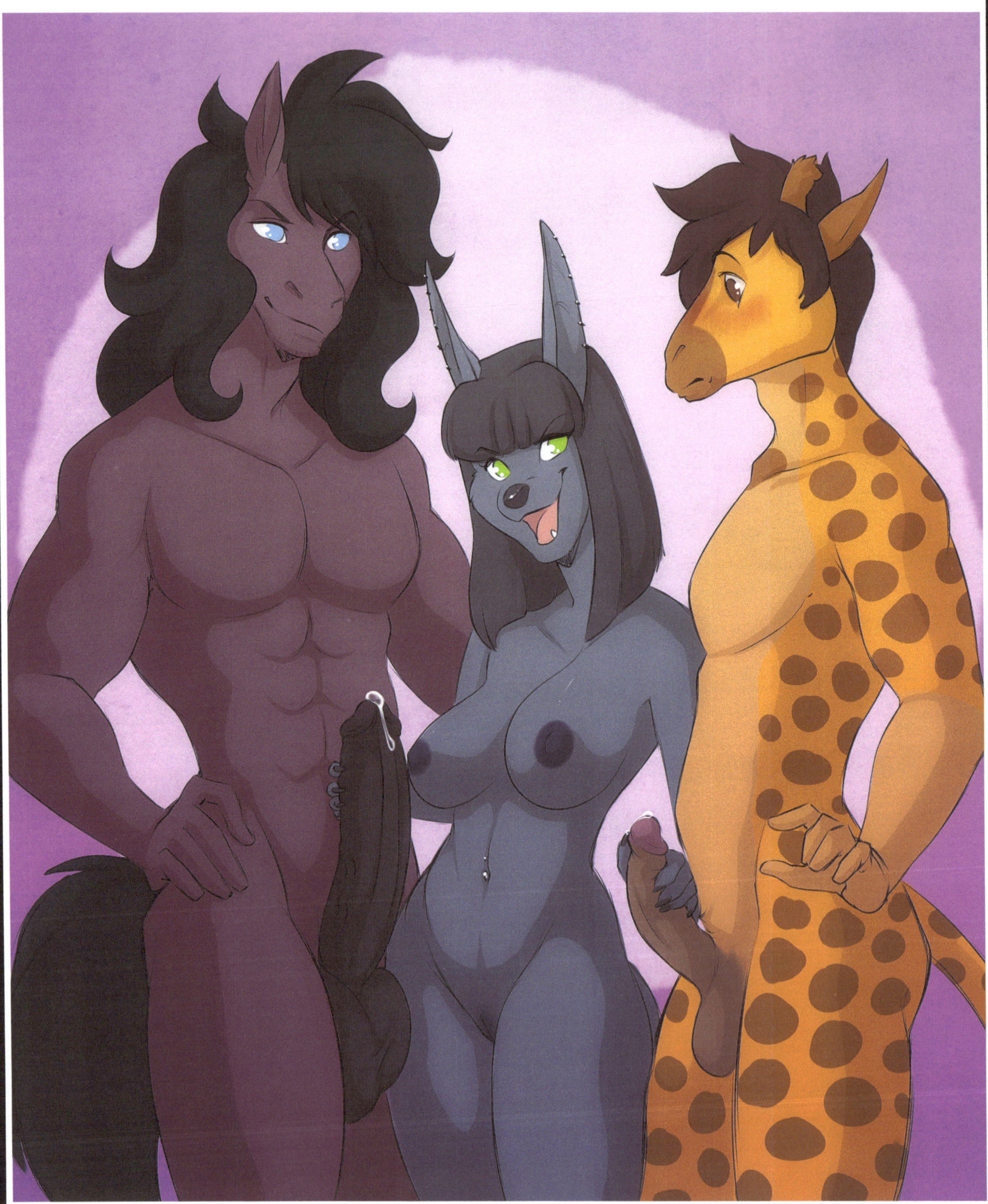

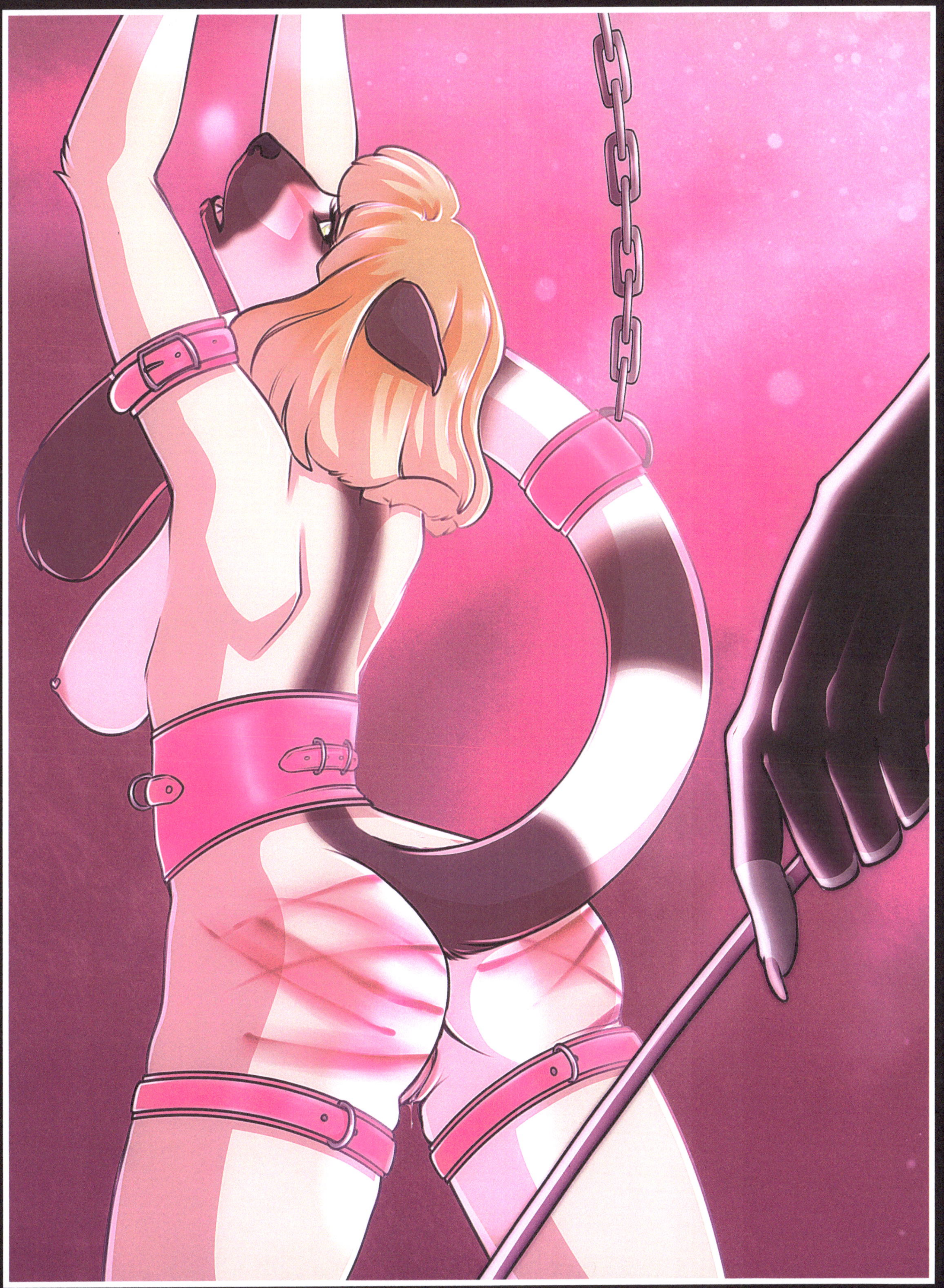

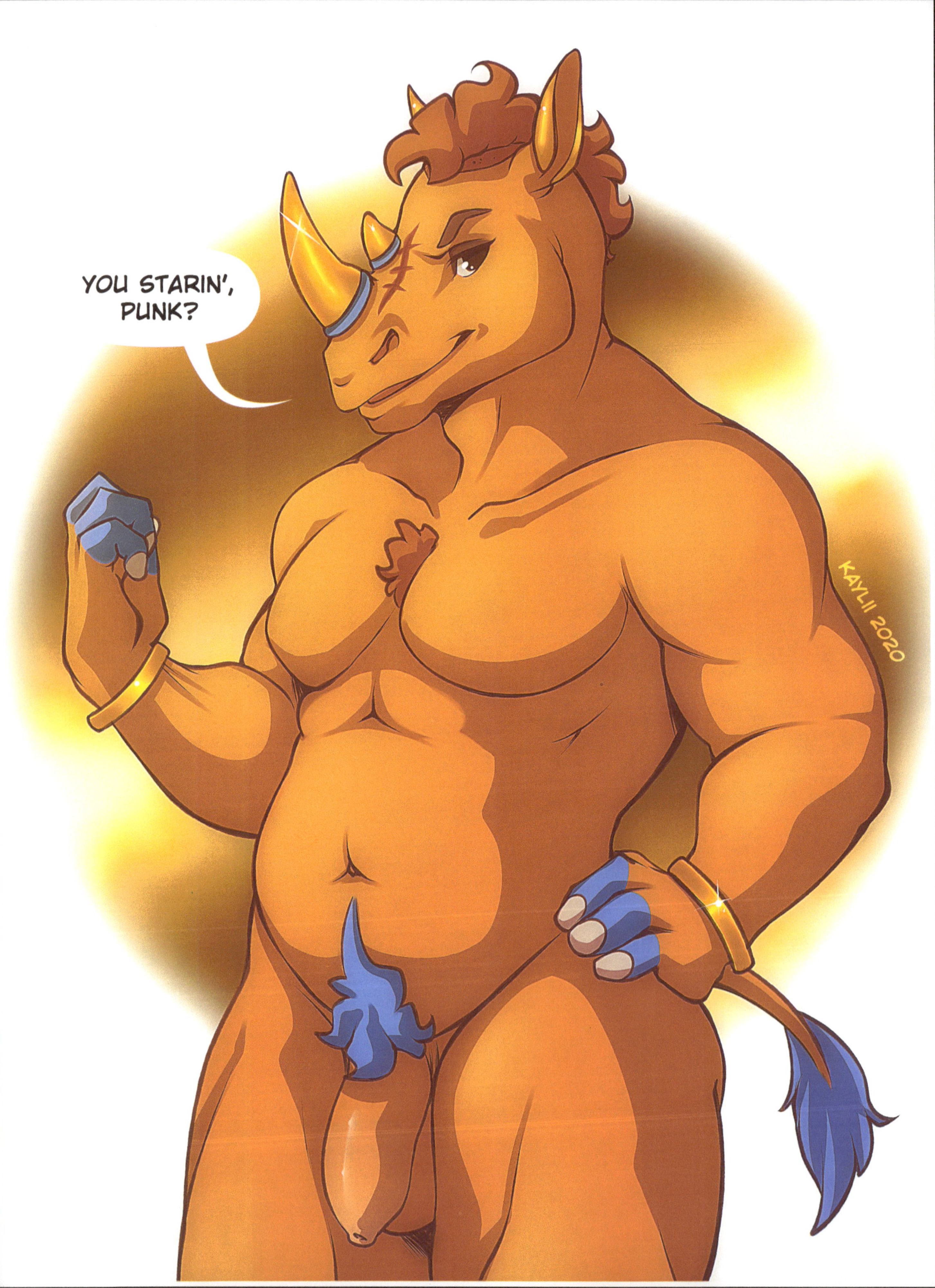
YOU STARIN', PUNK?
KAYLII 2020

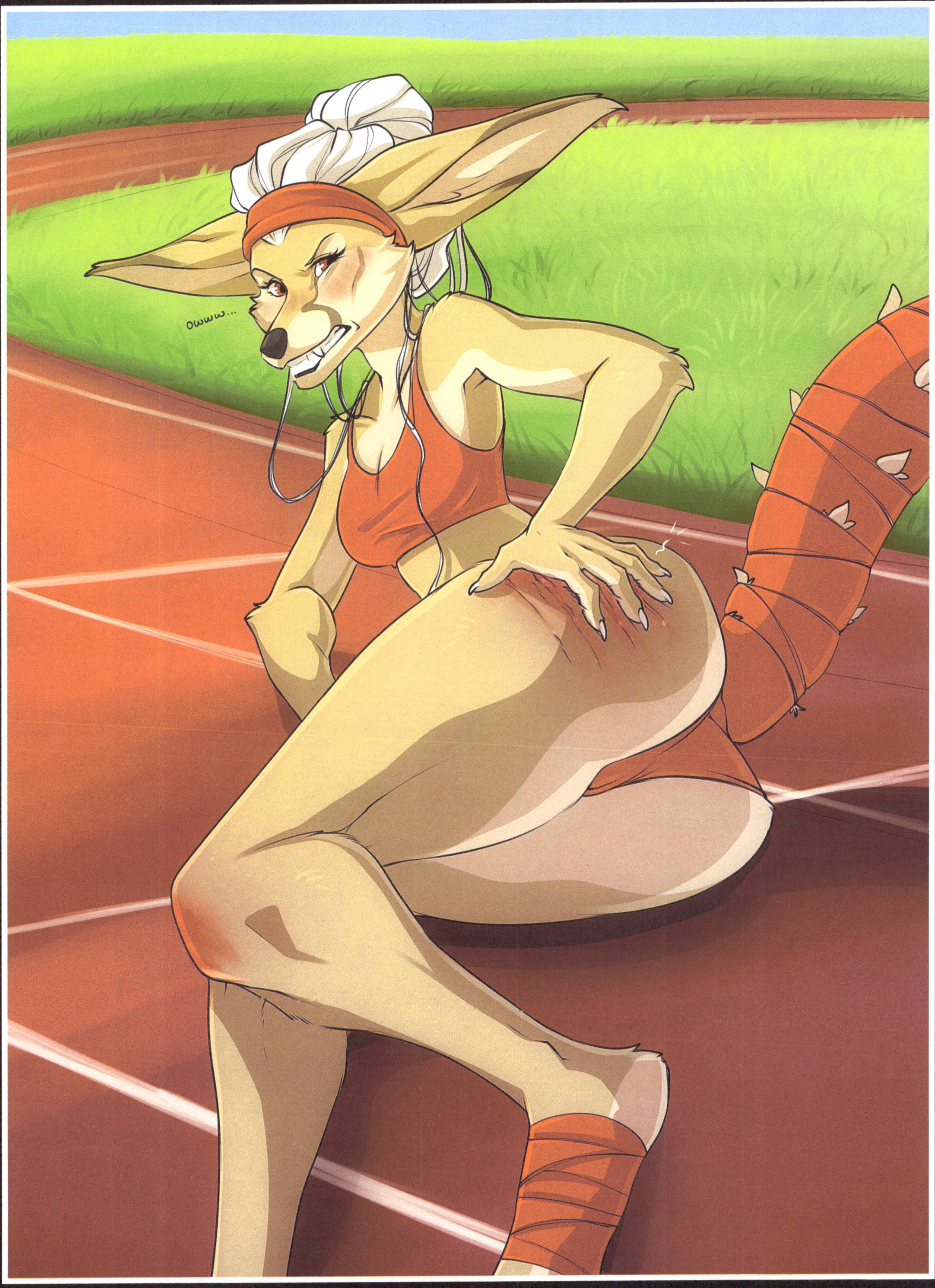
owww...

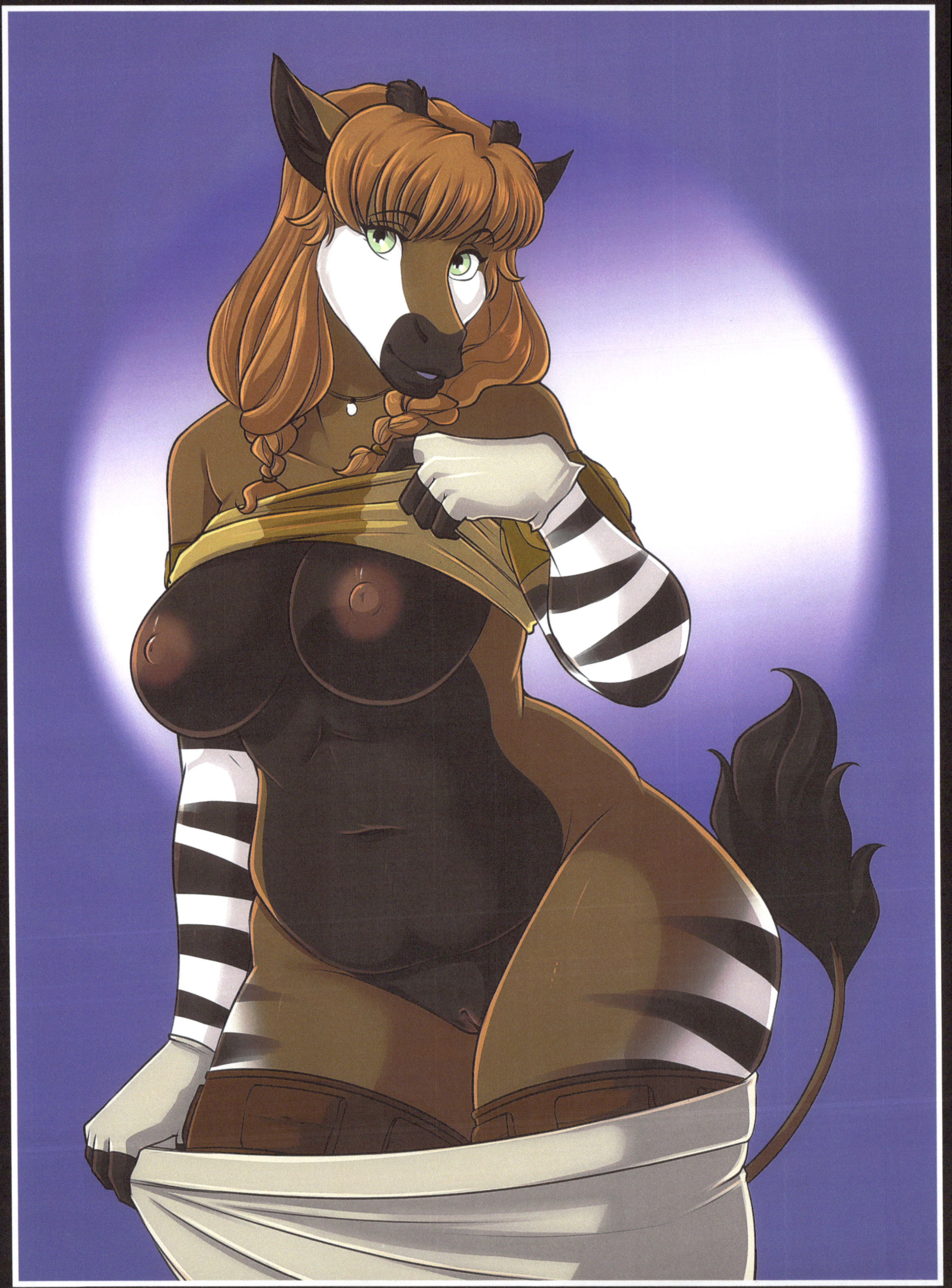

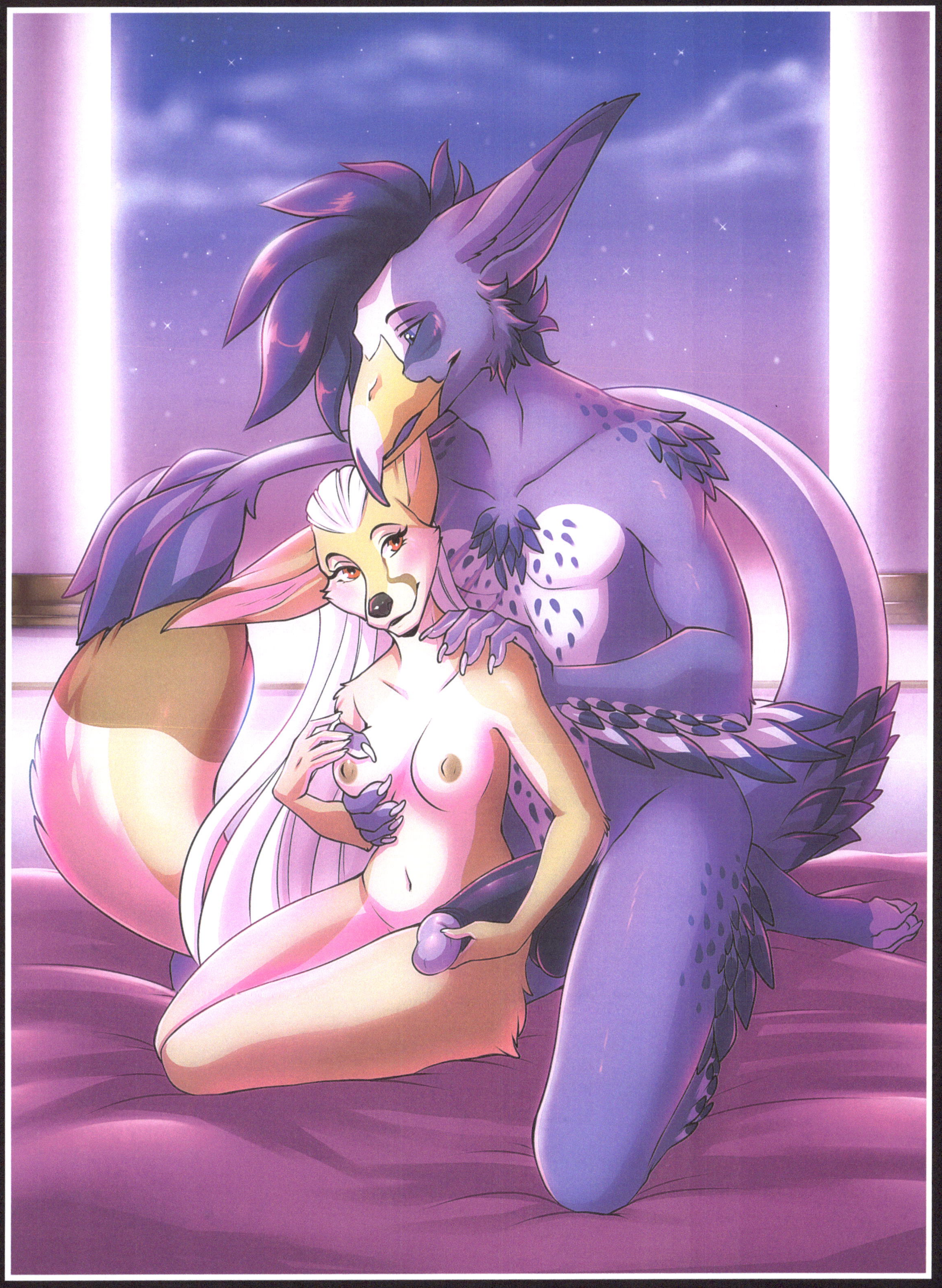

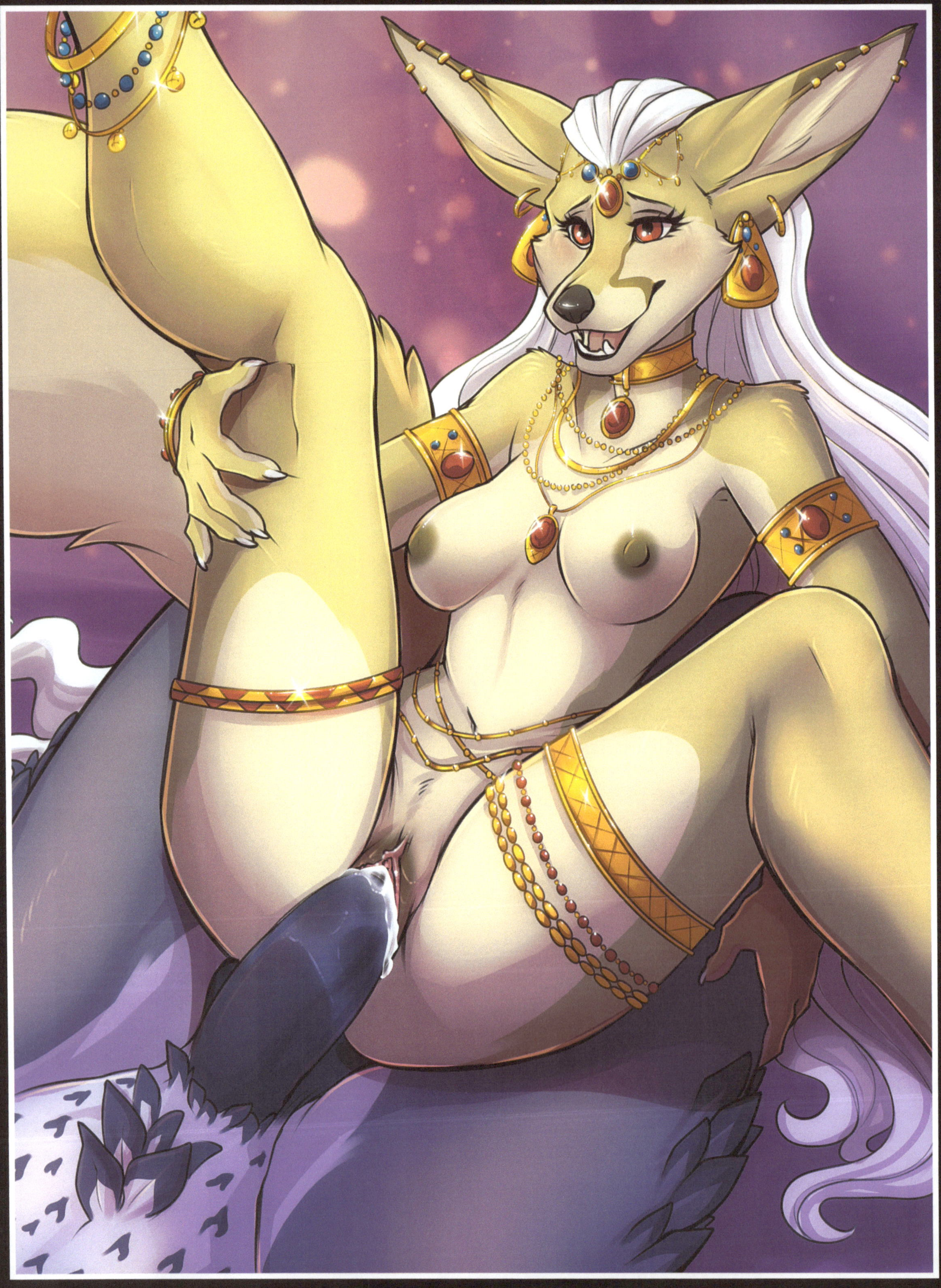

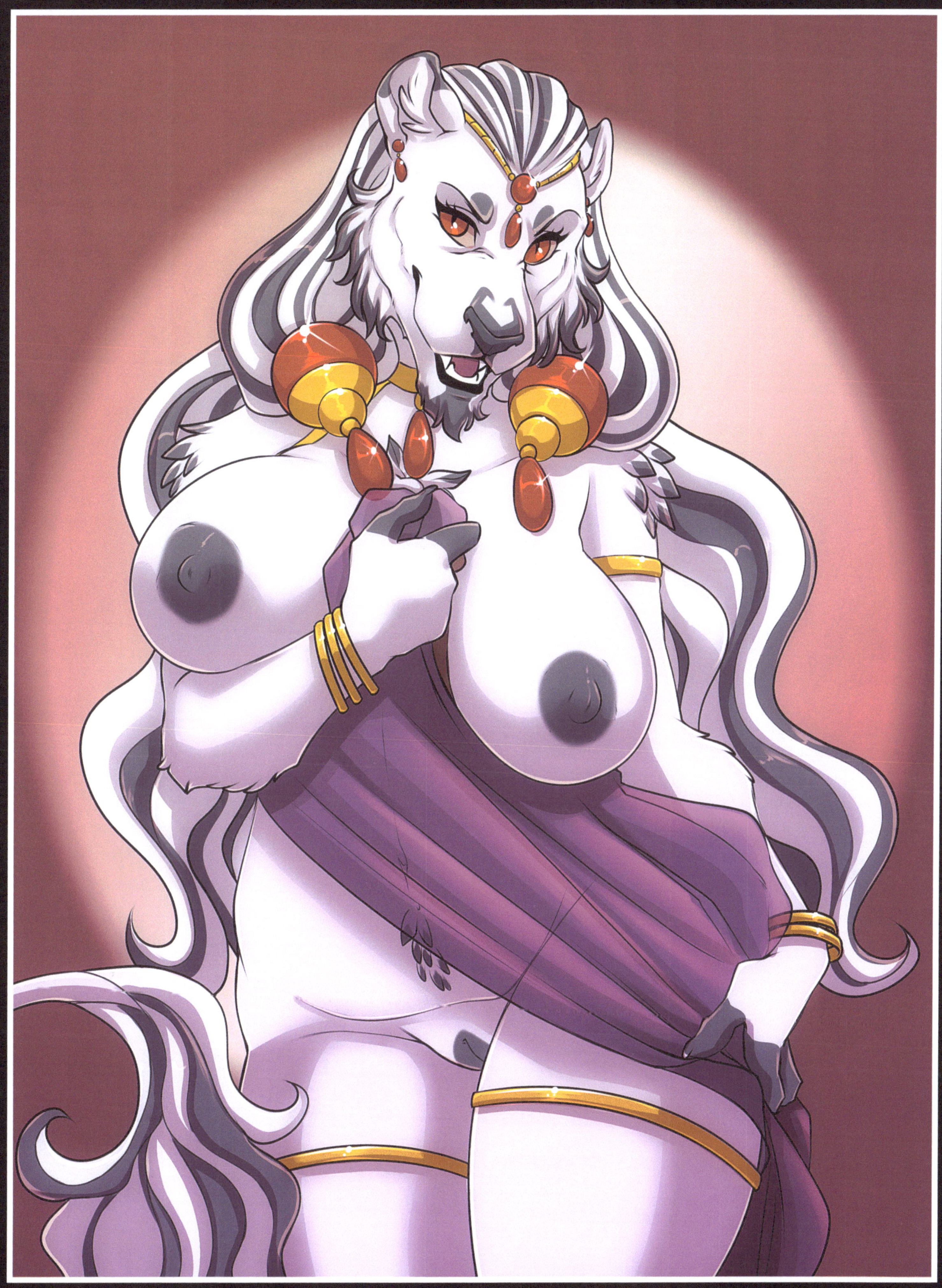

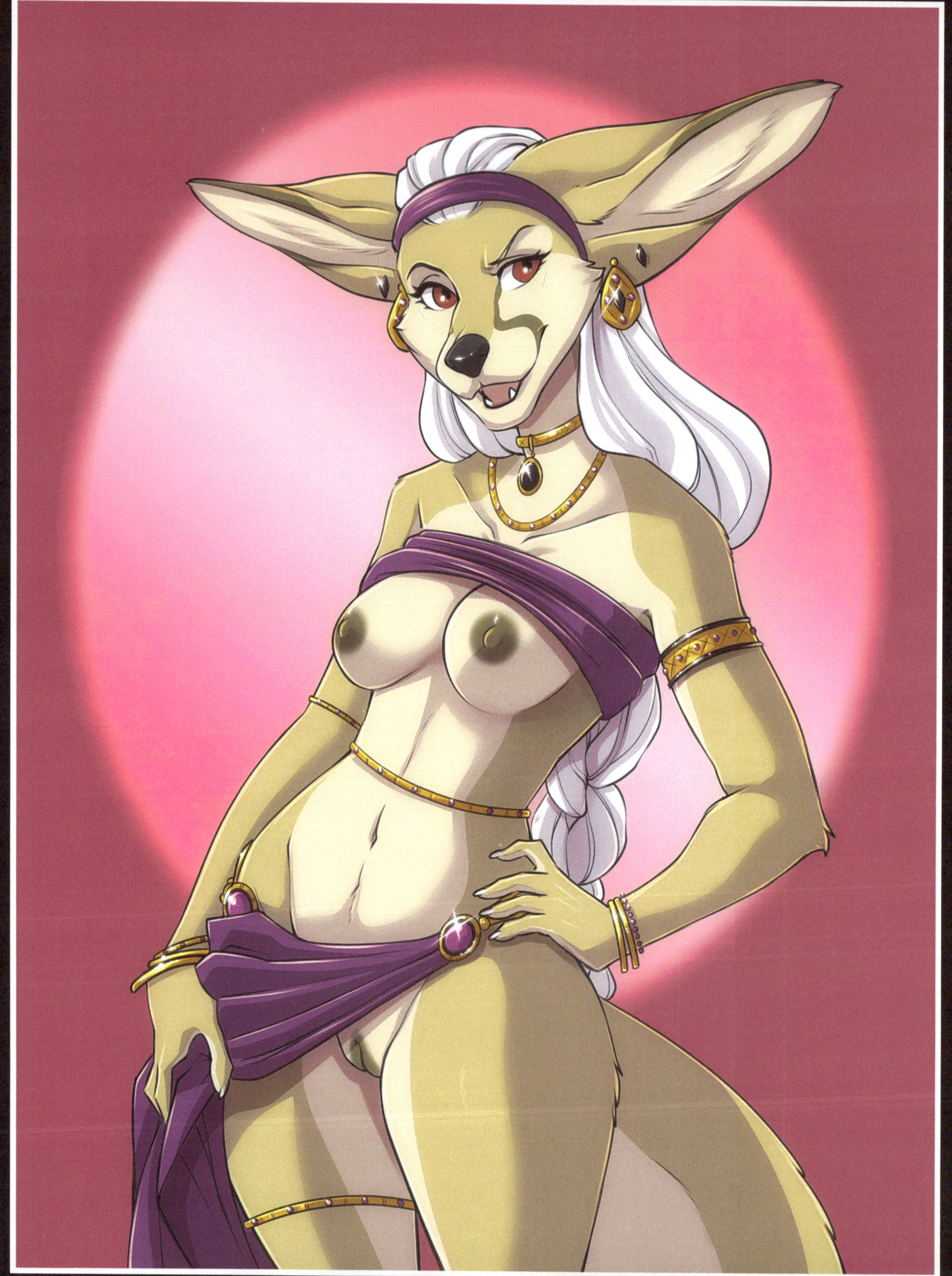

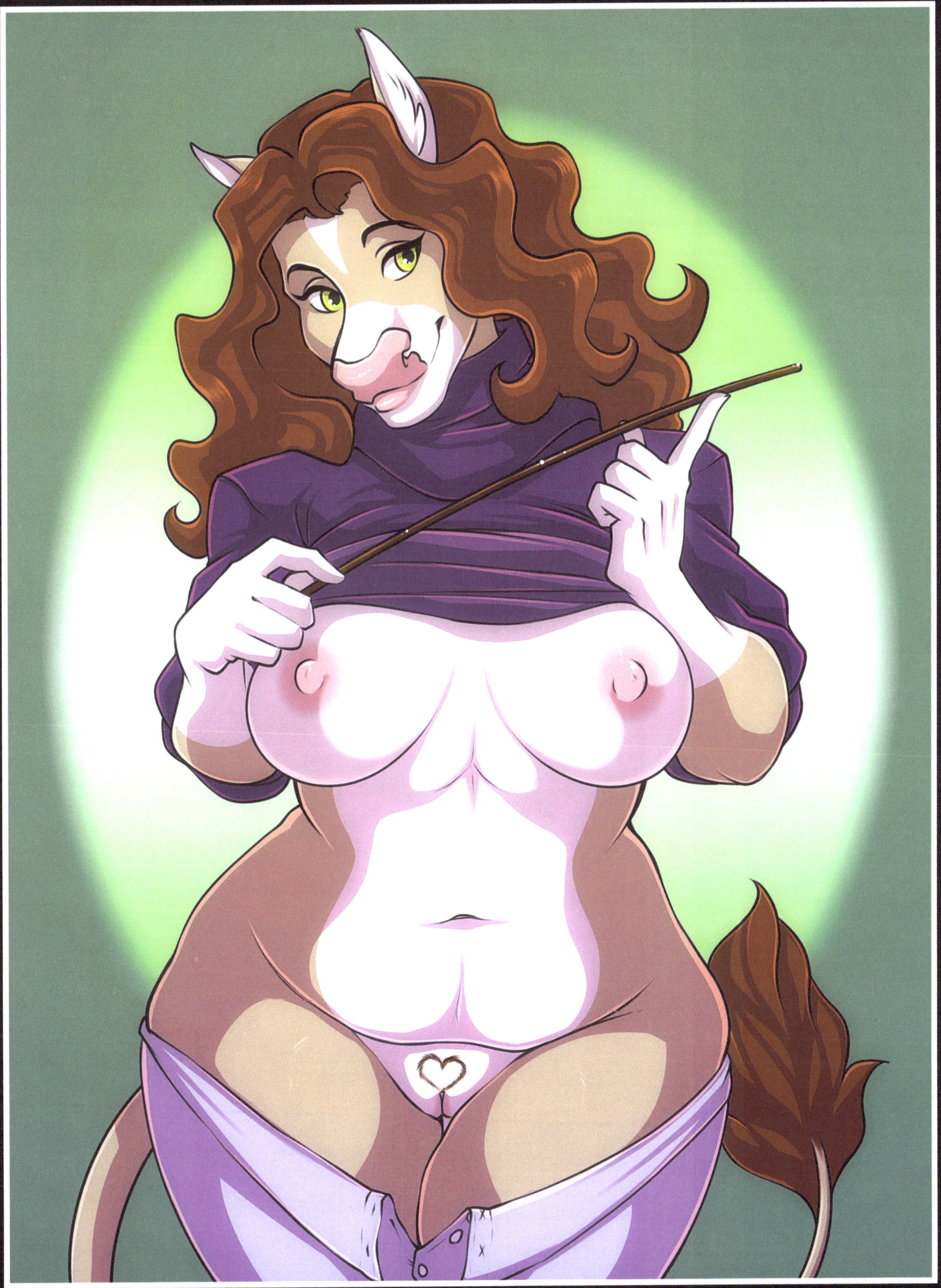

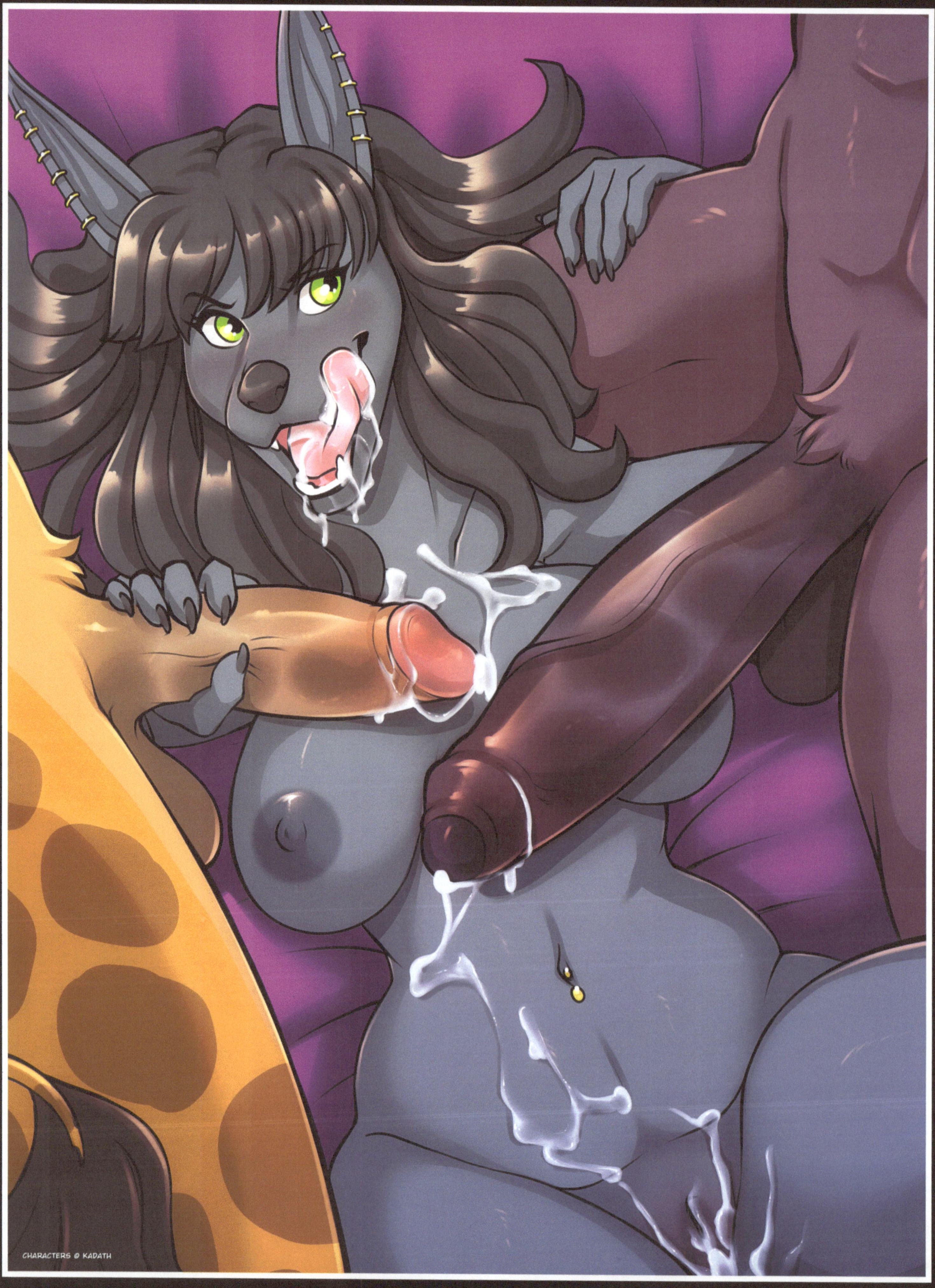
CHARACTERS © KADATH

www.ingramcontent.com/pod-product-compliance
Lightning Source LLC
LaVergne TN
LVHW070143110826
845147LV00002B/320
* 9 7 8 1 6 1 4 5 0 5 9 5 2 *